STAR BUS

ATTACK OF THE CLING-ONS

written by
Scott Ciencin

illustrated by
Jeff Crowther

STONE ARCH BOOKS
a capstone imprint

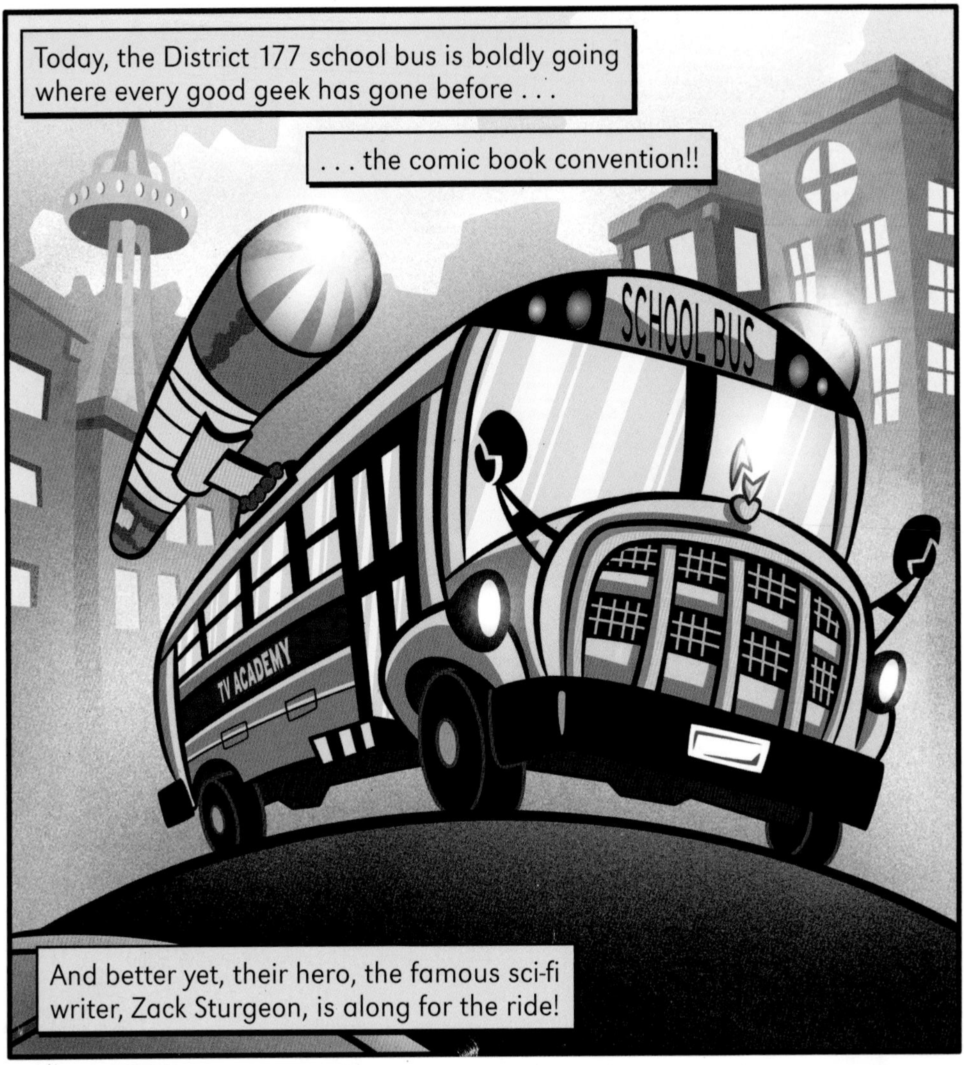

Today, the District 177 school bus is boldly going where every good geek has gone before . . .
. . . the comic book convention!!
SCHOOL BUS
TV ACADEMY
And better yet, their hero, the famous sci-fi writer, Zack Sturgeon, is along for the ride!

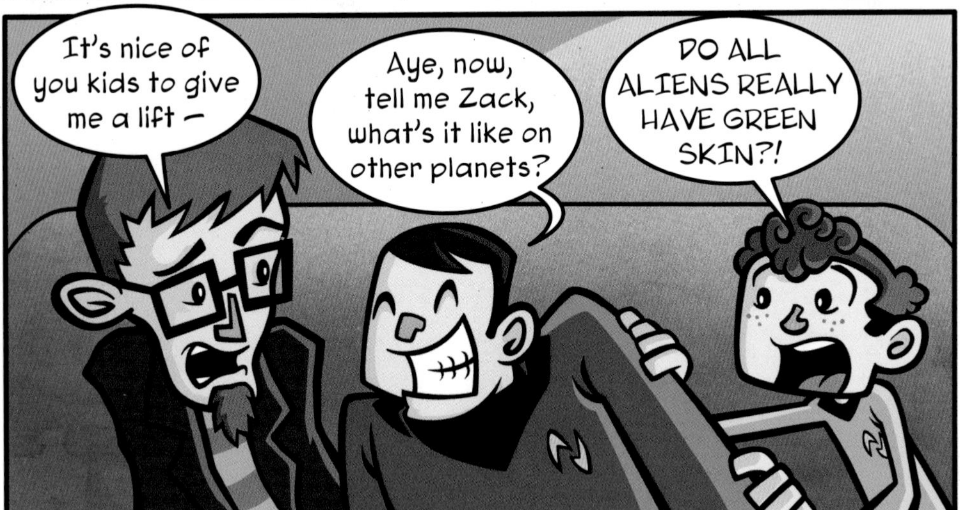

It's nice of you kids to give me a lift —
Aye, now, tell me Zack, what's it like on other planets?
DO ALL ALIENS REALLY HAVE GREEN SKIN?!

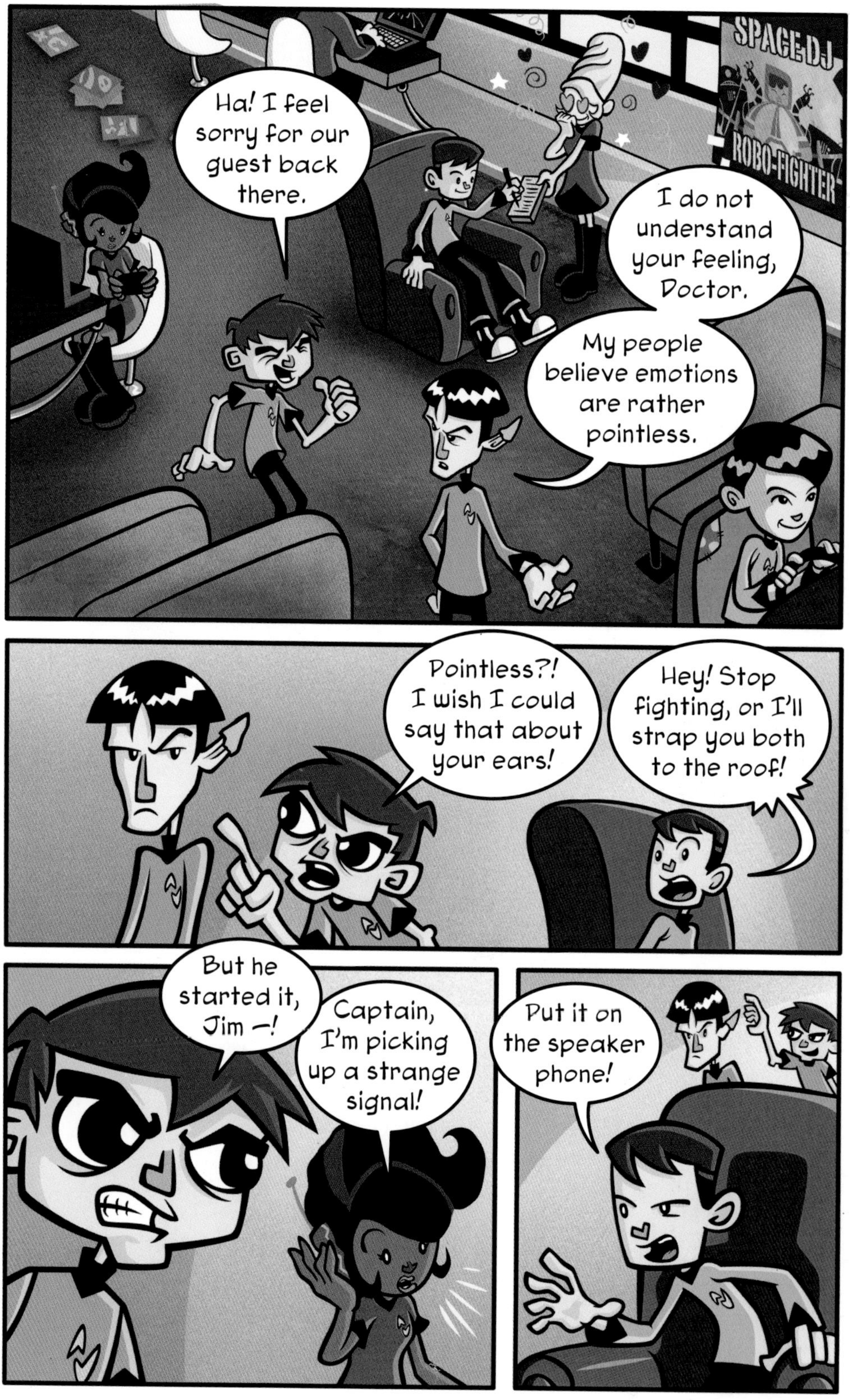

Ha! I feel sorry for our guest back there.
I do not understand your feeling, Doctor.
My people believe emotions are rather pointless.
SPACE DJ
ROBO-FIGHTER
Pointless?! I wish I could say that about your ears!
Hey! Stop fighting, or I'll strap you both to the roof!
But he started it, Jim —!
Captain, I'm picking up a strange signal!
Put it on the speaker phone!

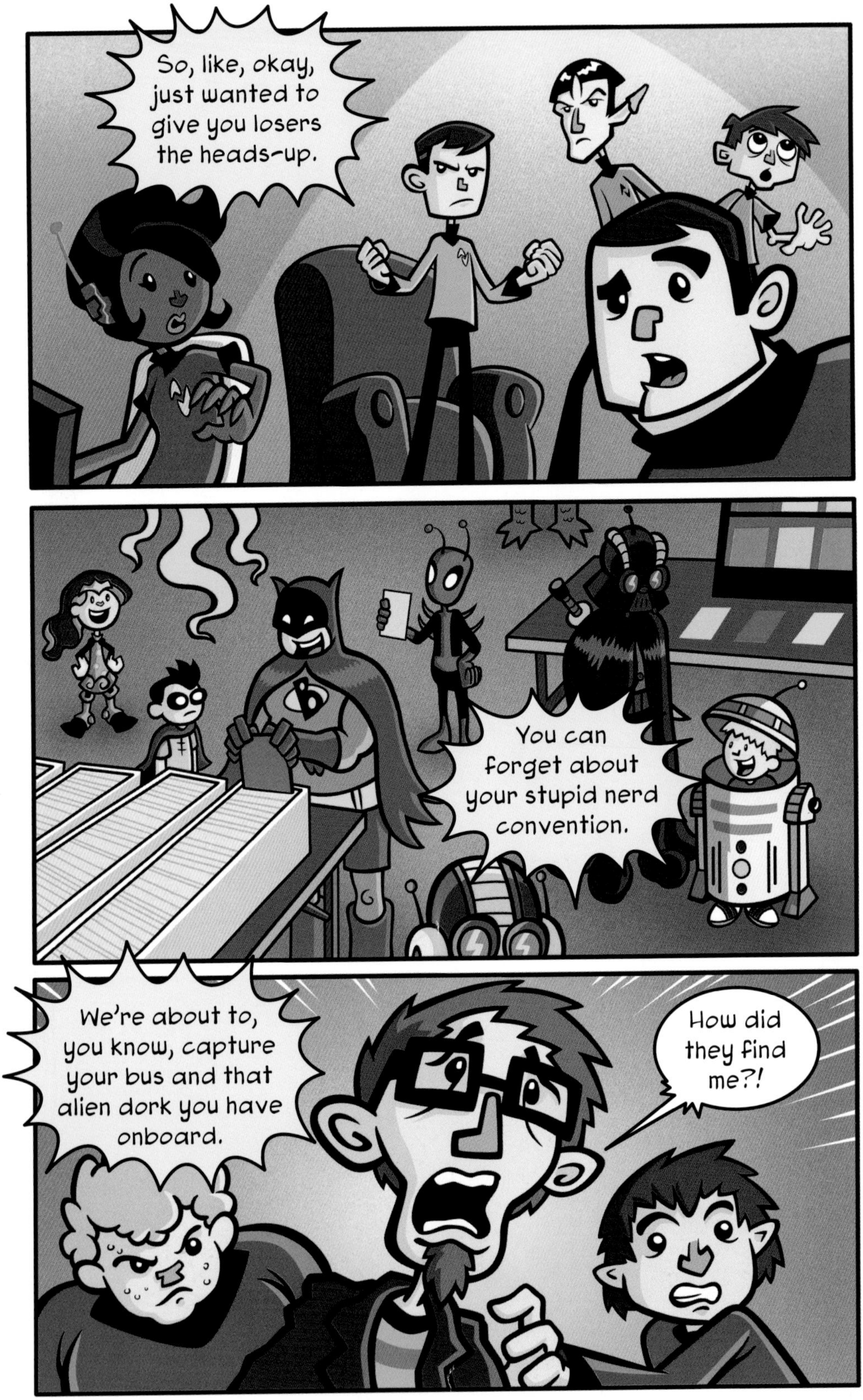

So, like, okay, just wanted to give you losers the heads-up.
You can forget about your stupid nerd convention.
We're about to, you know, capture your bus and that alien dork you have onboard.
How did they find me?!

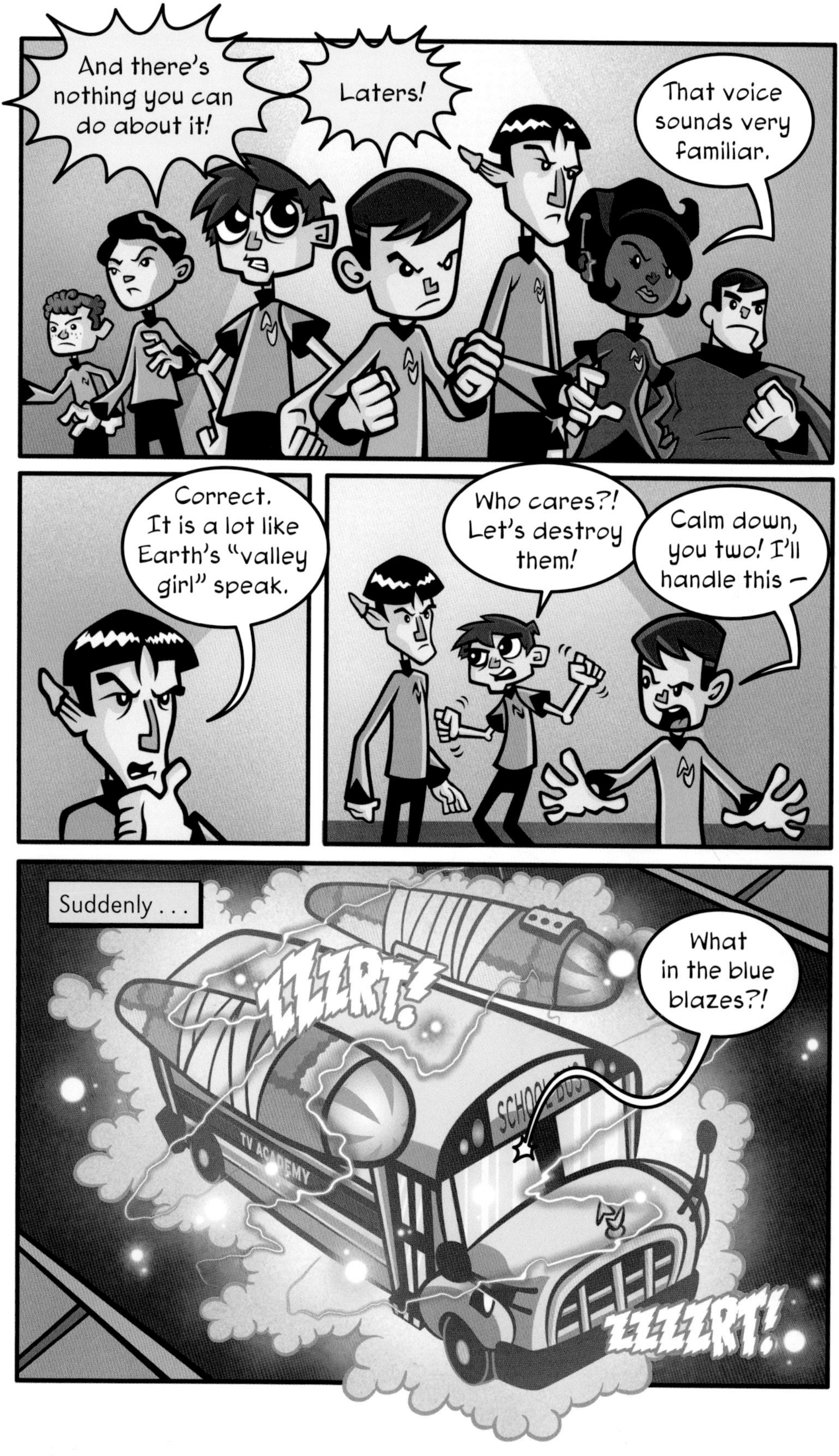
And there's nothing you can do about it!
Laters!
That voice sounds very familiar.
Correct. It is a lot like Earth's "valley girl" speak.
Who cares?! Let's destroy them!
Calm down, you two! I'll handle this —
Suddenly . . .
ZZZRT!
What in the blue blazes?!
SCHOOL BUS
TV ACADEMY
ZZZZRT!

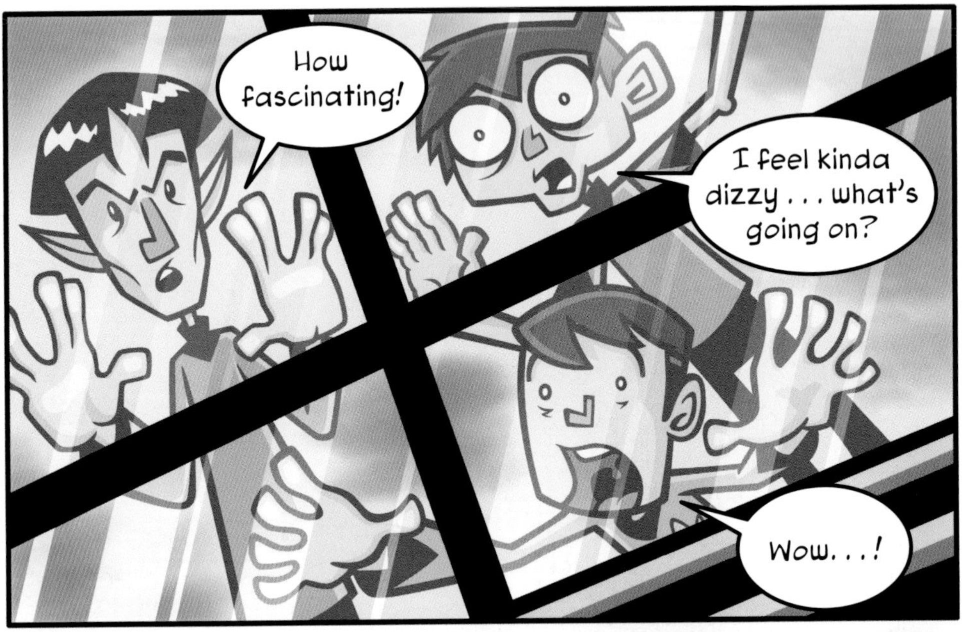
How fascinating!
I feel kinda dizzy . . . what's going on?
Wow. . .!

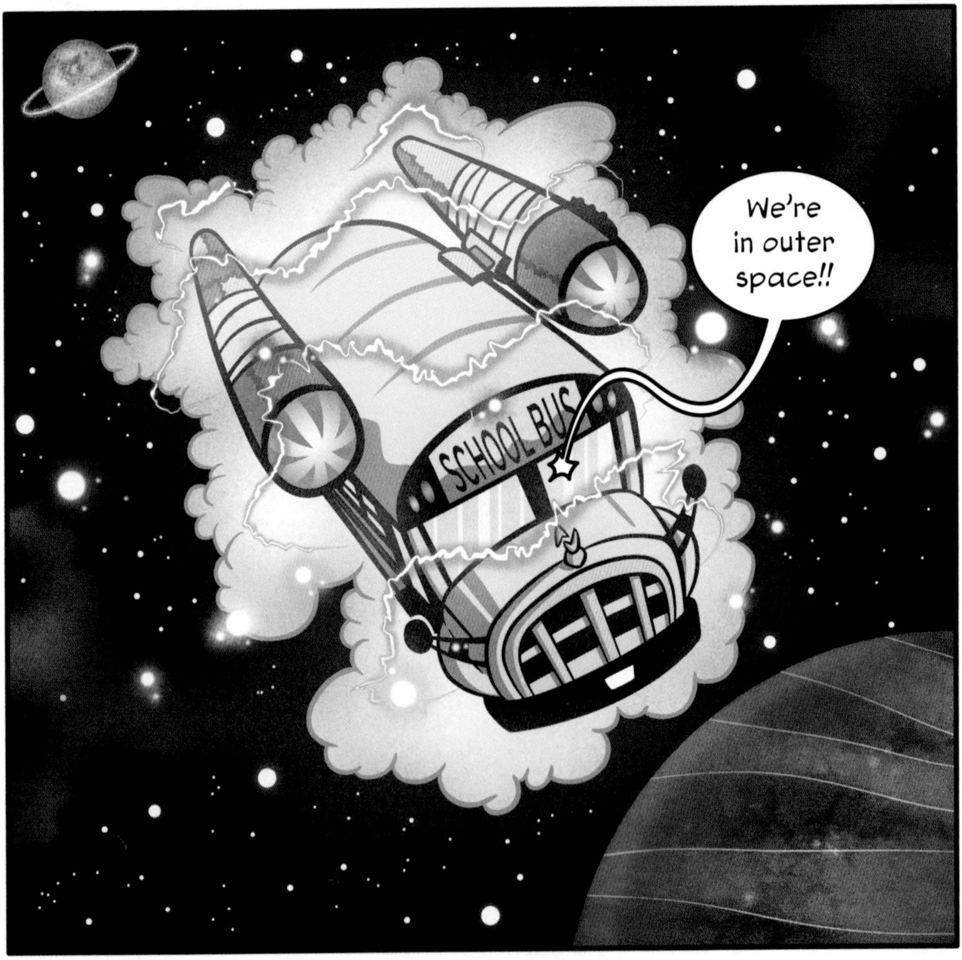
We're in outer space!!
SCHOOL BUS

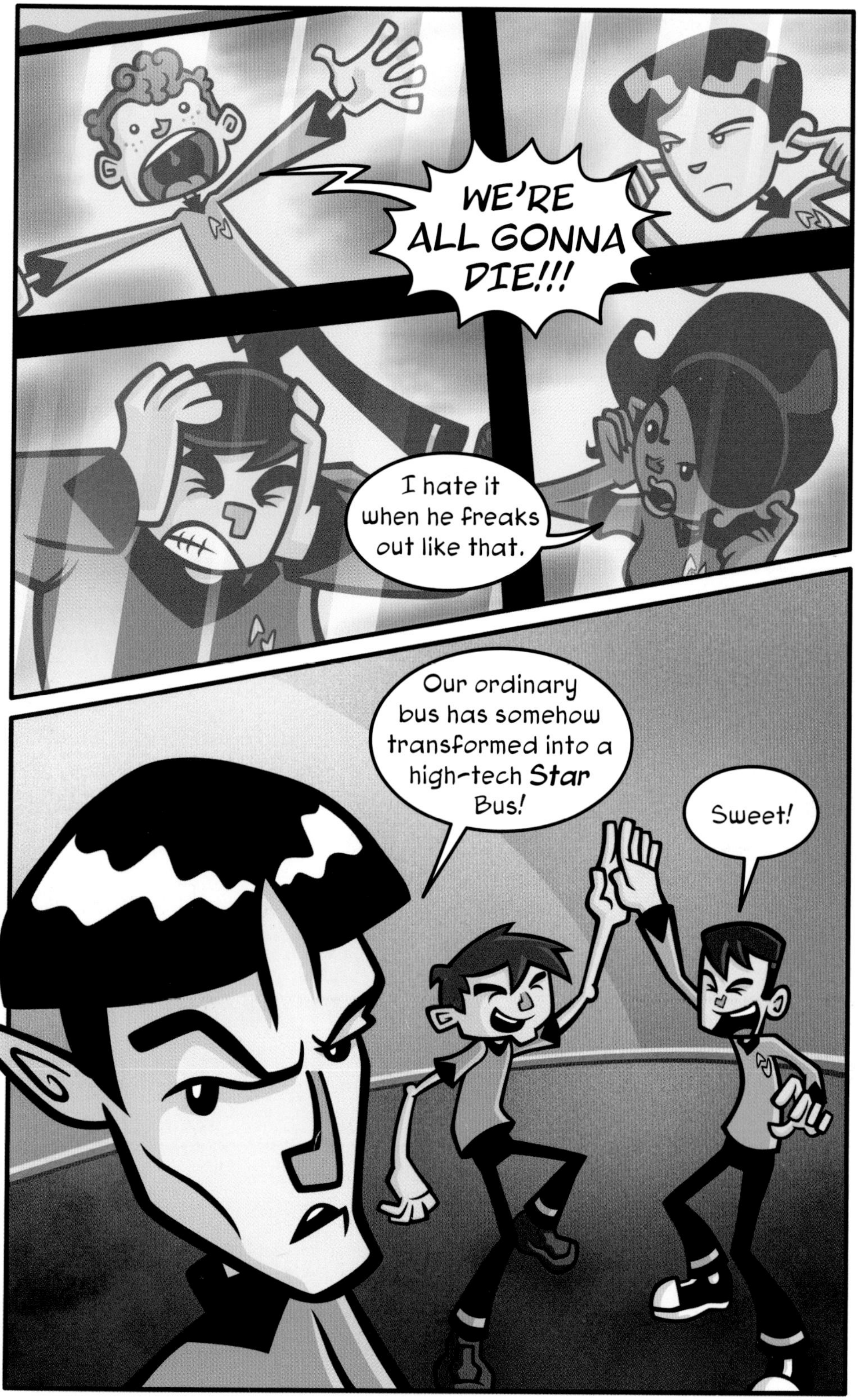
WE'RE ALL GONNA DIE!!!
I hate it when he freaks out like that.
Our ordinary bus has somehow transformed into a high-tech Star Bus!
Sweet!

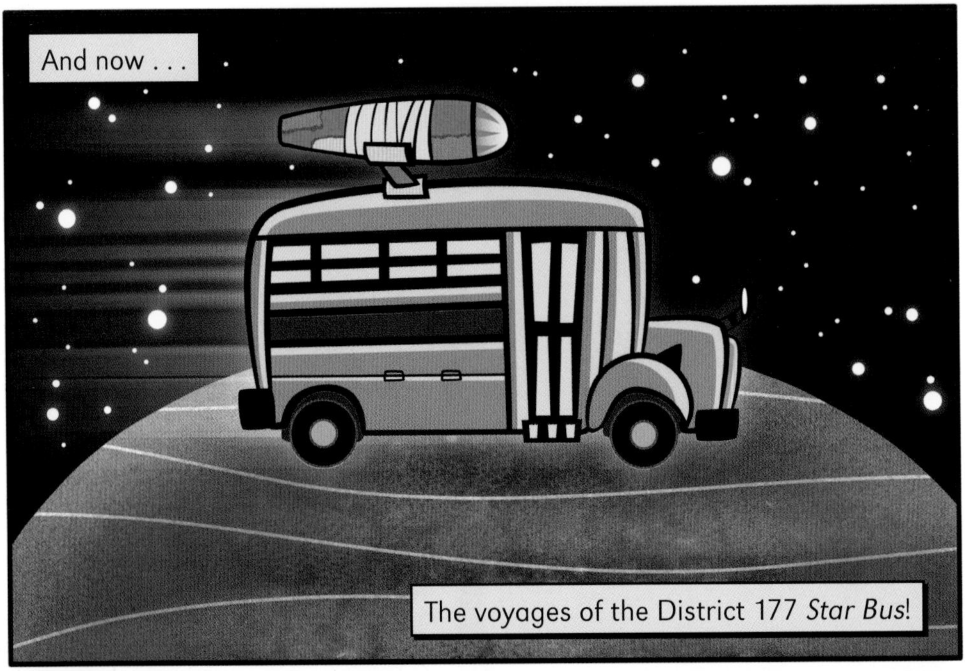
And now . . .
The voyages of the District 177 *Star Bus*!

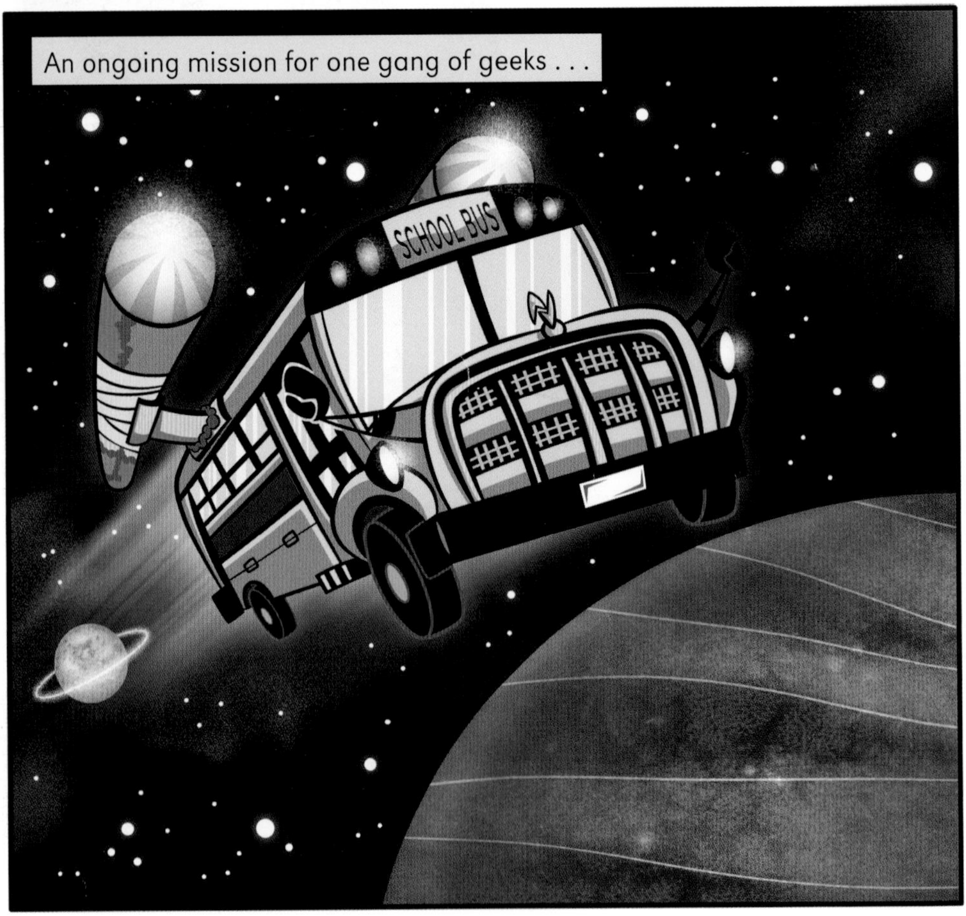
An ongoing mission for one gang of geeks . . .
SCHOOL BUS

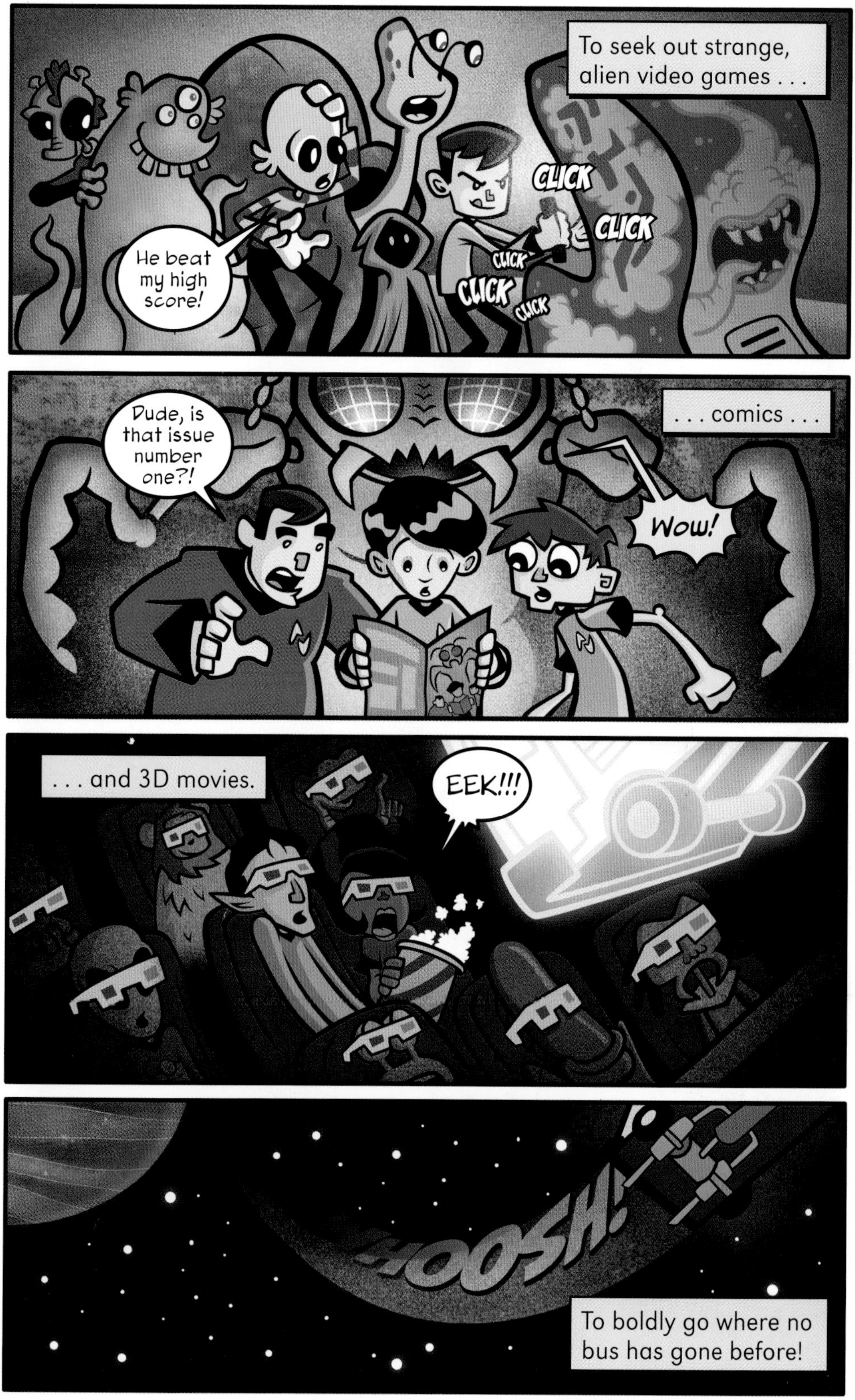
To seek out strange, alien video games . . .
He beat my high score!
CLICK
CLICK
CLICK
CLICK
CLICK
. . . comics . . .
Dude, is that issue number one?!
Wow!
. . . and 3D movies.
EEK!!!
HOOSH!
To boldly go where no bus has gone before!

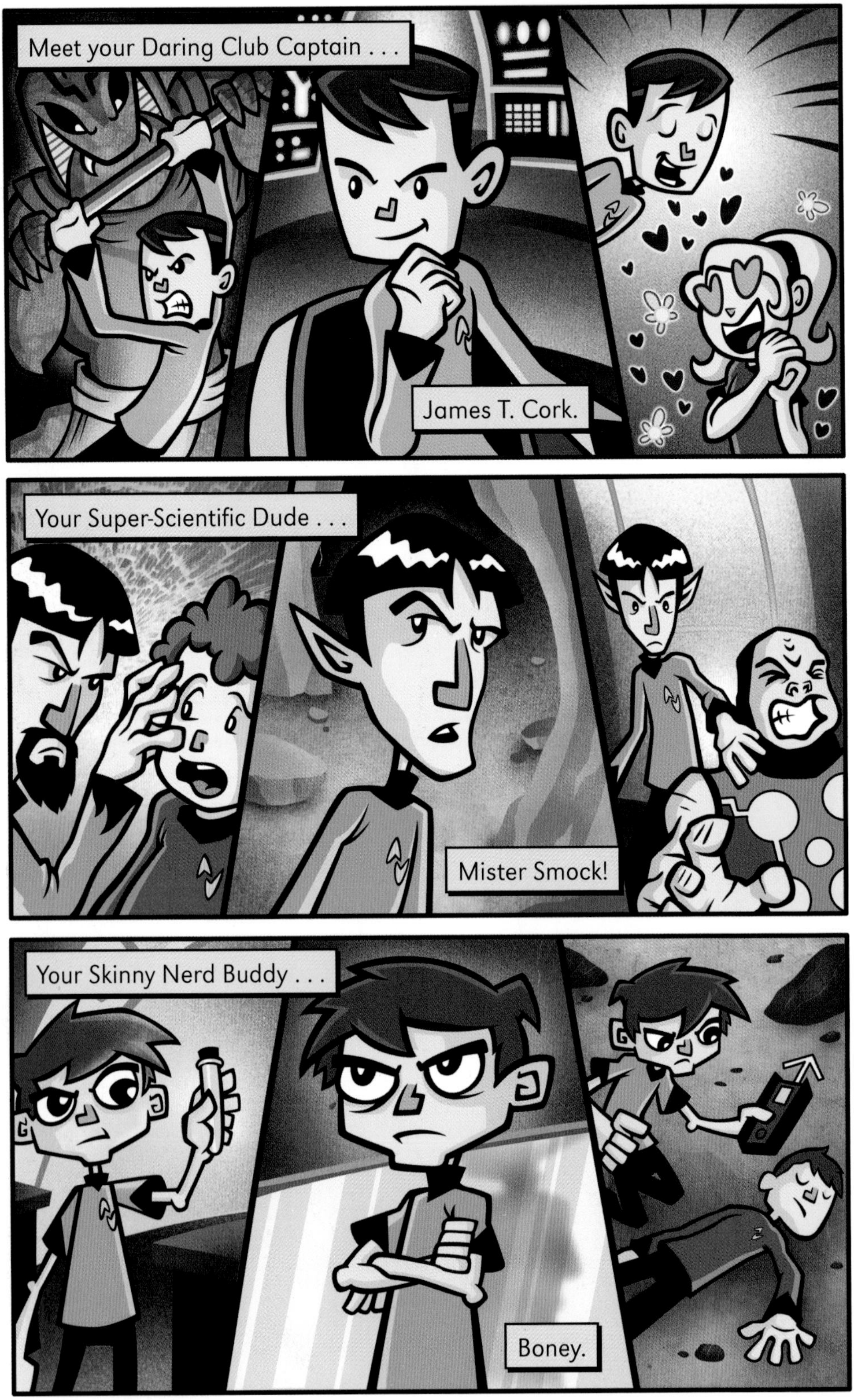
Meet your Daring Club Captain . . .
James T. Cork.
Your Super-Scientific Dude . . .
Mister Smock!
Your Skinny Nerd Buddy . . .
Boney.

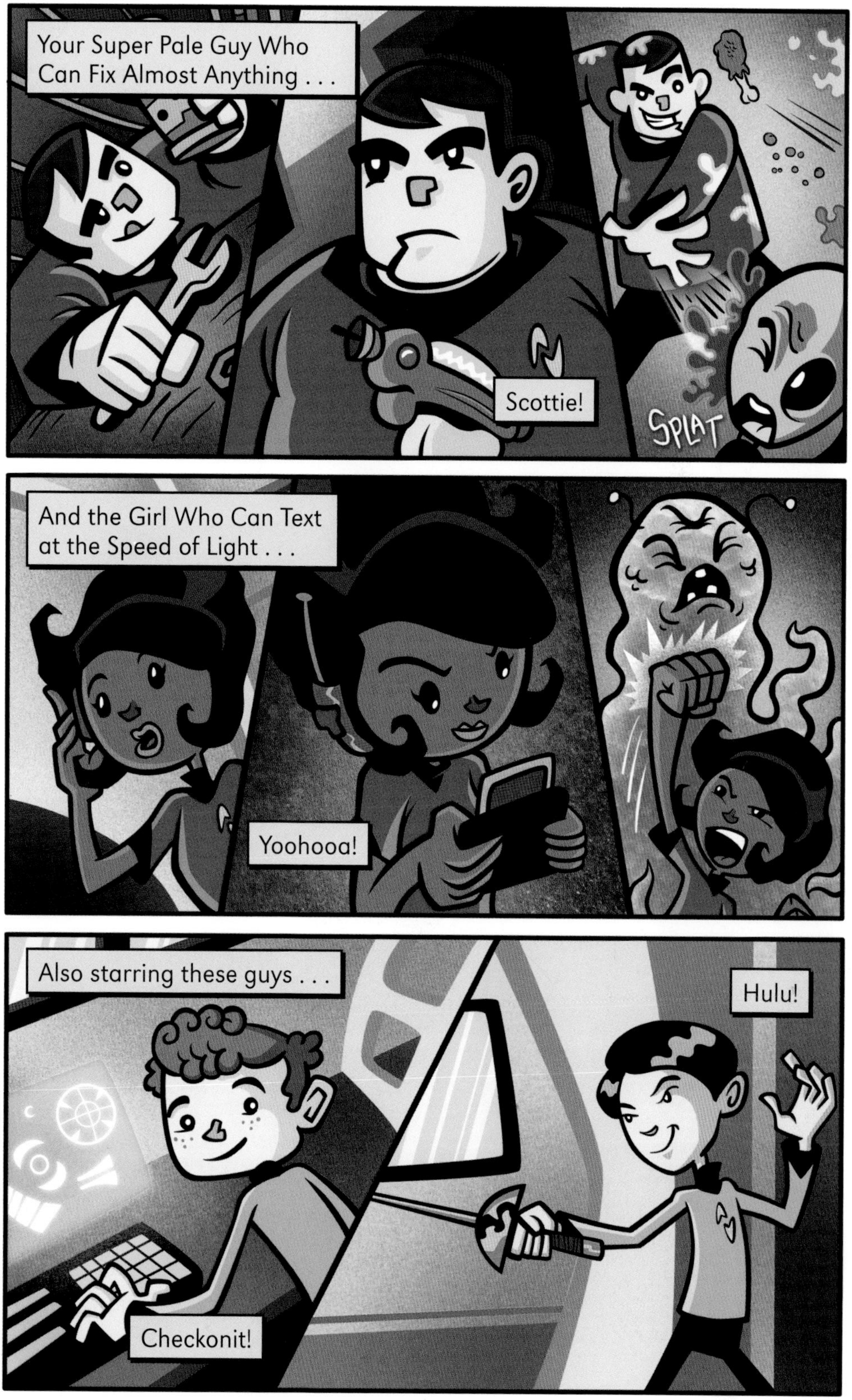
Your Super Pale Guy Who Can Fix Almost Anything . . .
Scottie!
SPLAT
And the Girl Who Can Text at the Speed of Light . . .
Yoohooa!
Also starring these guys . . .
Checkonit!
Hulu!

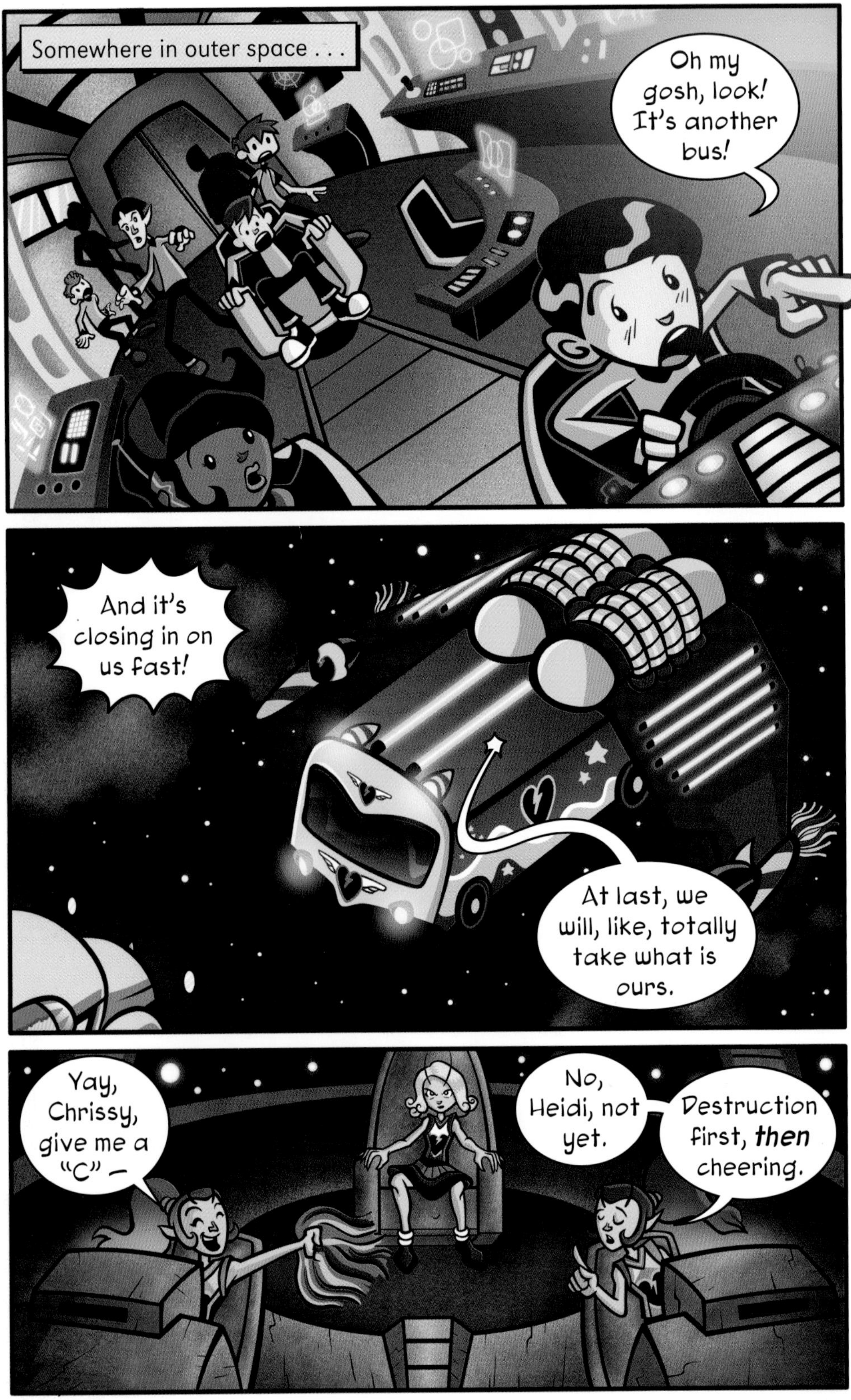
Somewhere in outer space . . .
Oh my gosh, look! It's another bus!
And it's closing in on us fast!
At last, we will, like, totally take what is ours.
Yay, Chrissy, give me a "C" —
No, Heidi, not yet.
Destruction first, *then* cheering.

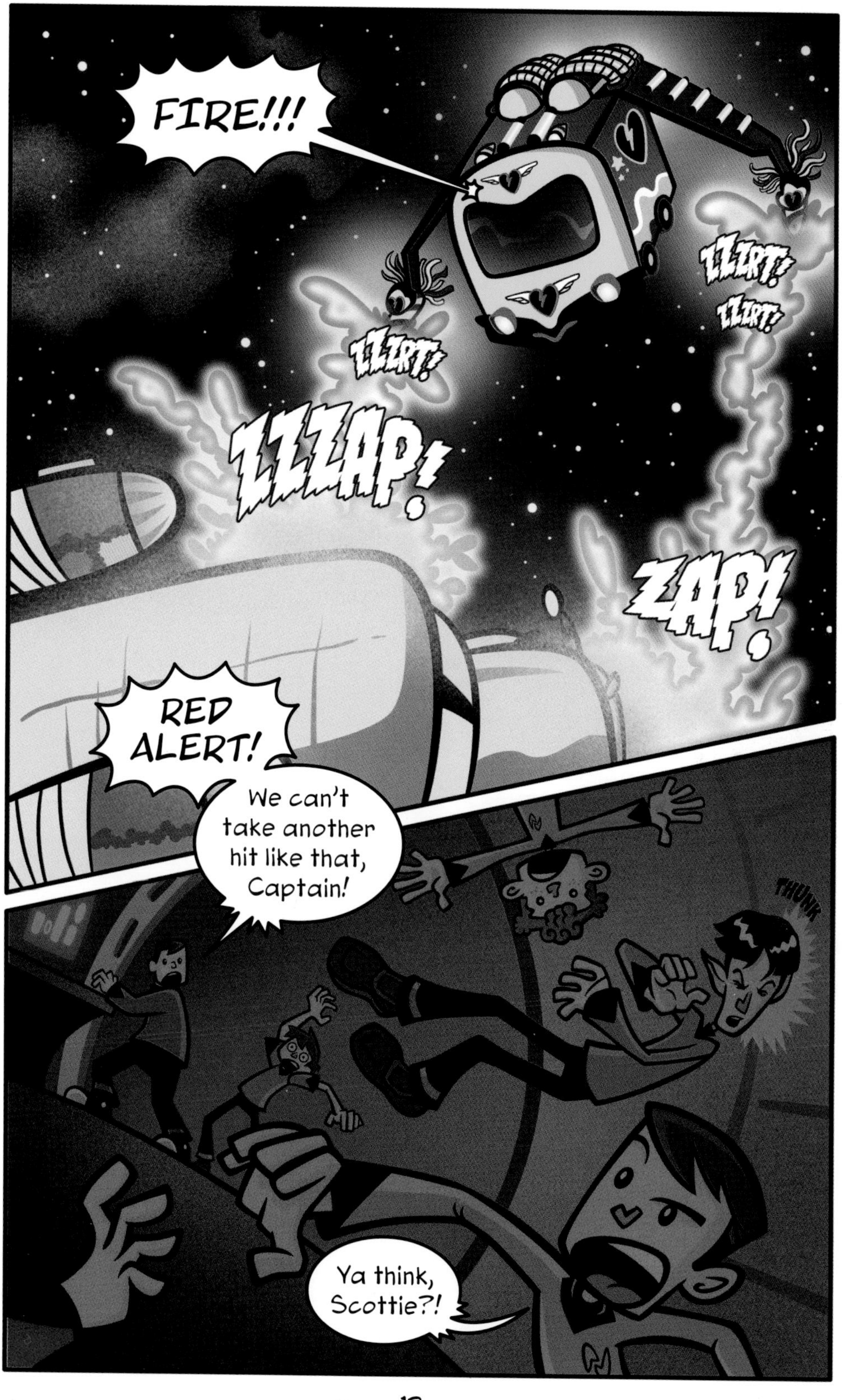
FIRE!!!
ZZZRT!
ZZZRT!
ZZZRT!
ZZZAP!
ZAP!
RED ALERT!
We can't take another hit like that, Captain!
THUNK
Ya think, Scottie?!

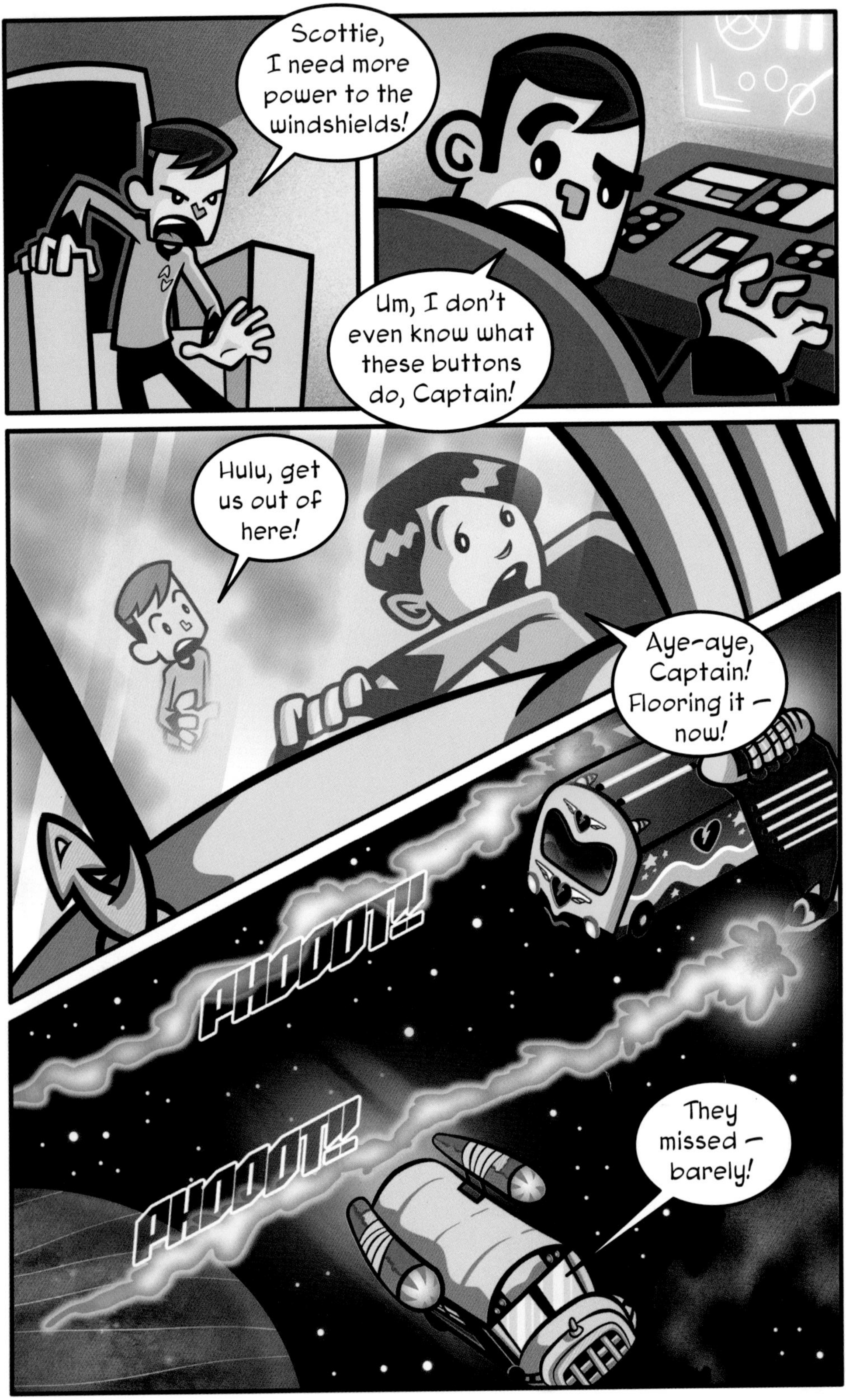
Scottie, I need more power to the windshields!
Um, I don't even know what these buttons do, Captain!
Hulu, get us out of here!
Aye-aye, Captain! Flooring it — now!
PHOOOT!!
PHOOOT!!
They missed — barely!

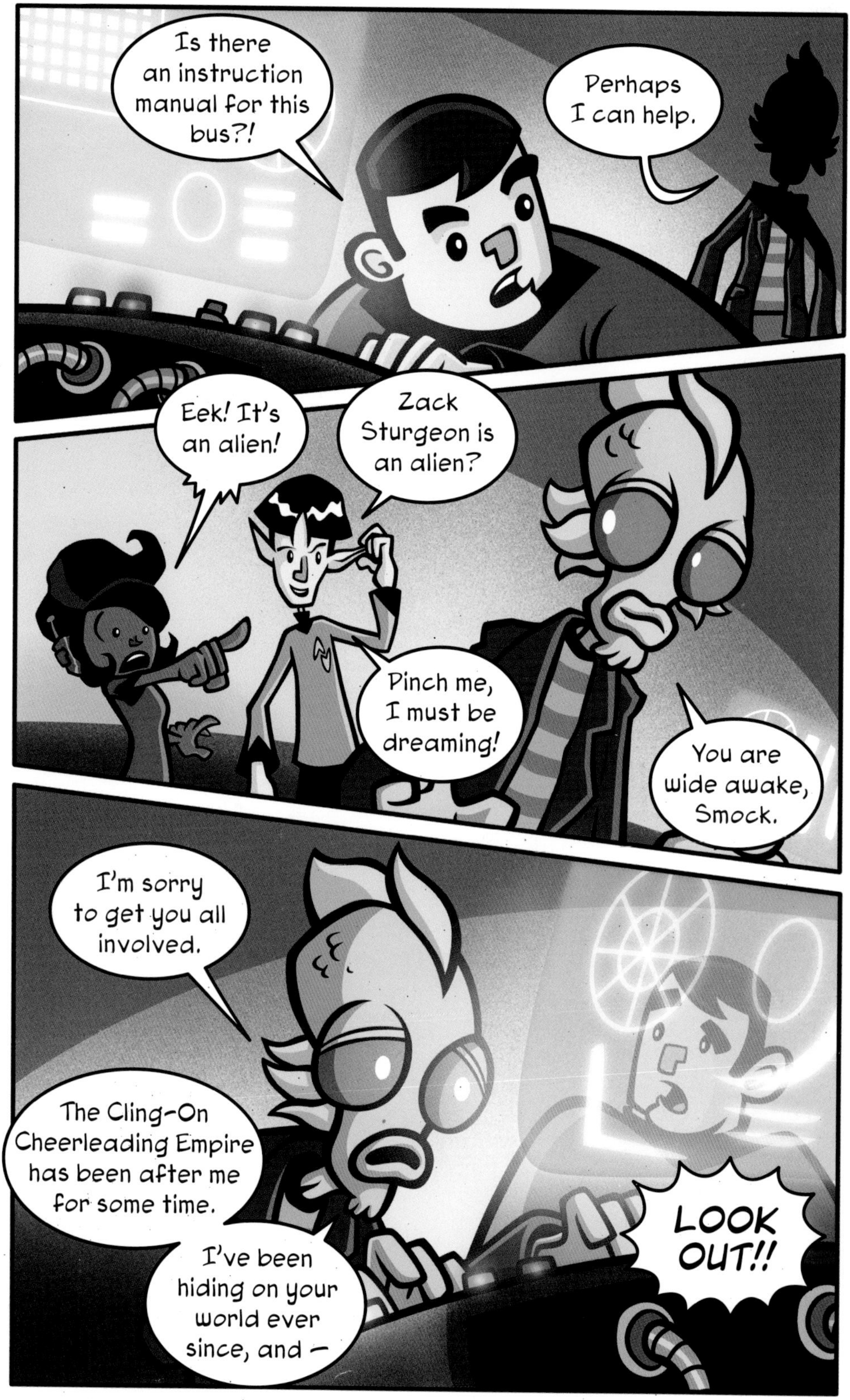
Is there an instruction manual for this bus?!
Perhaps I can help.
Eek! It's an alien!
Zack Sturgeon is an alien?
Pinch me, I must be dreaming!
You are wide awake, Smock.
I'm sorry to get you all involved.
The Cling-On Cheerleading Empire has been after me for some time.
I've been hiding on your world ever since, and —
LOOK OUT!!

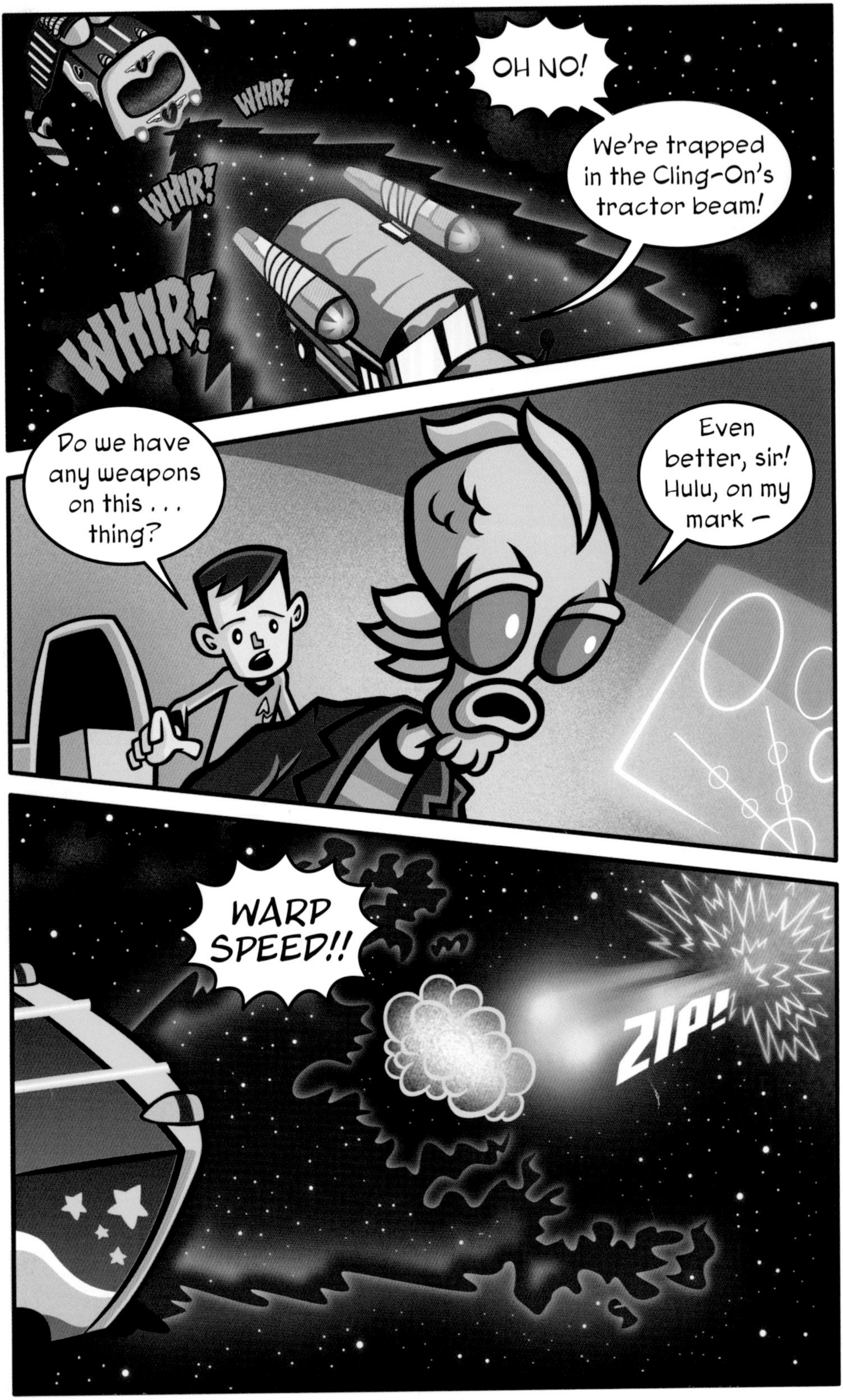

OH NO!
We're trapped in the Cling-On's tractor beam!
WHIR!
WHIR!
WHIR!
Do we have any weapons on this . . . thing?
Even better, sir! Hulu, on my mark —
WARP SPEED!!
ZIP!

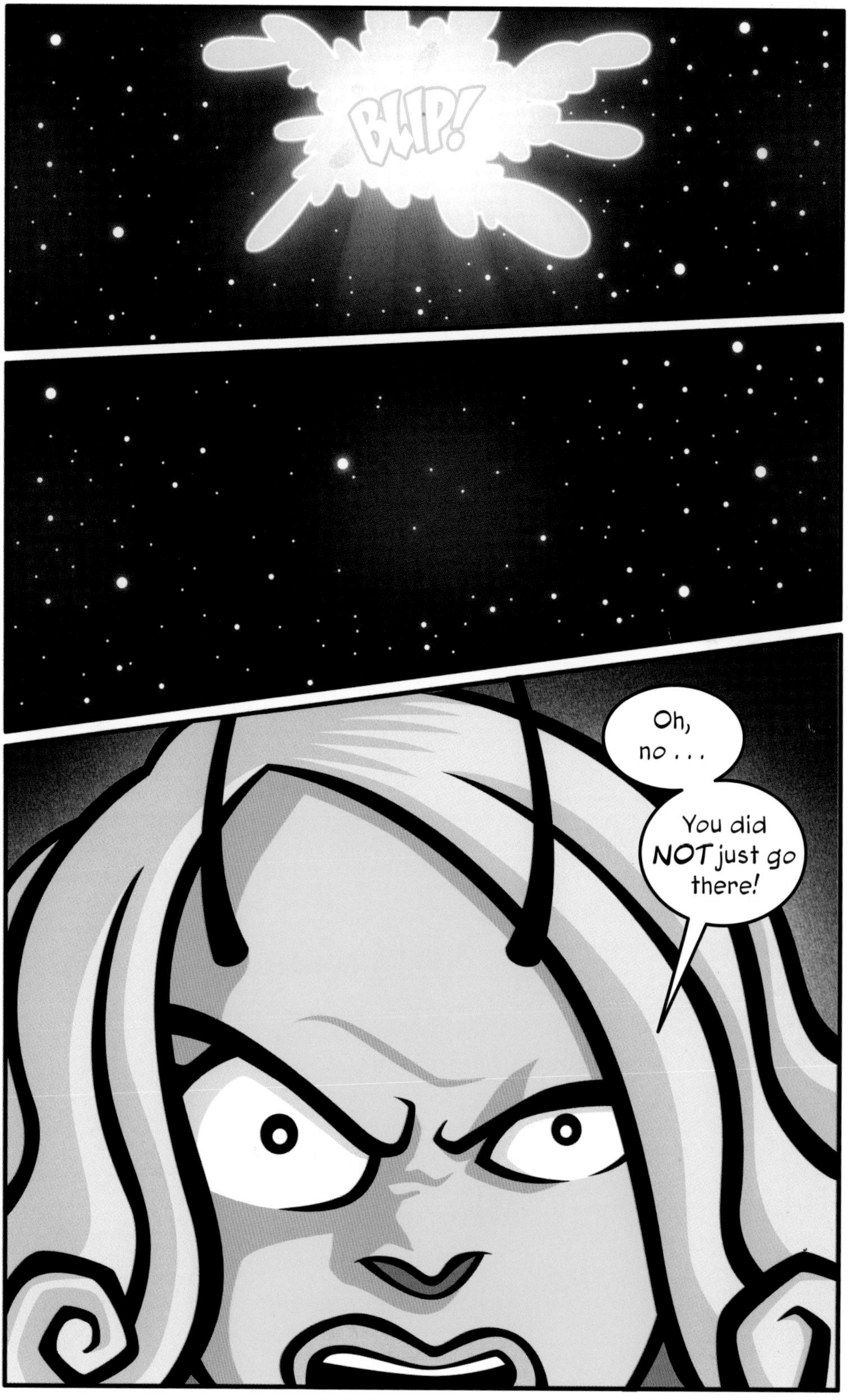
BLIP!
Oh, no . . .
You did NOT just go there!

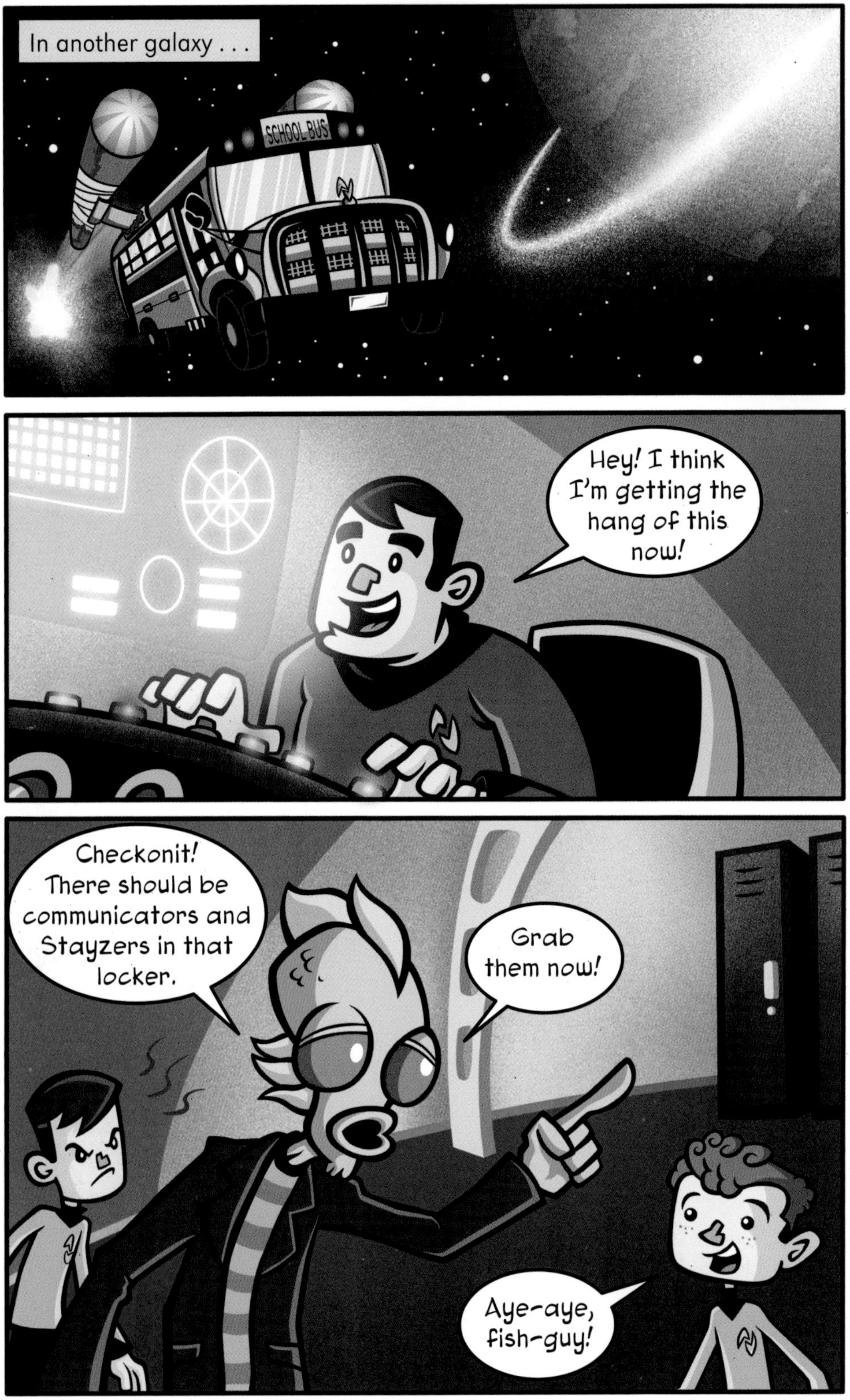
In another galaxy . . .
SCHOOL BUS
Hey! I think I'm getting the hang of this now!
Checkonit! There should be communicators and Stayzers in that locker.
Grab them now!
Aye-aye, fish-guy!

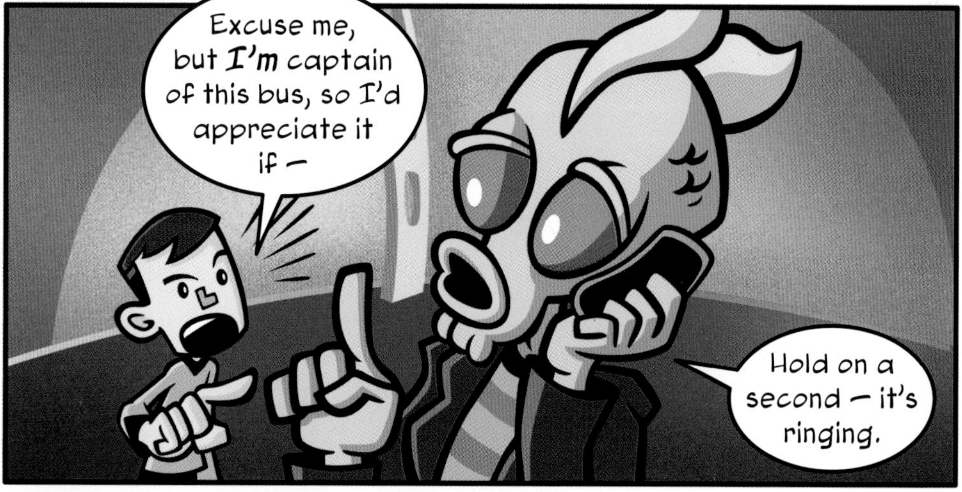
Excuse me, but I'm captain of this bus, so I'd appreciate it if —
Hold on a second — it's ringing.

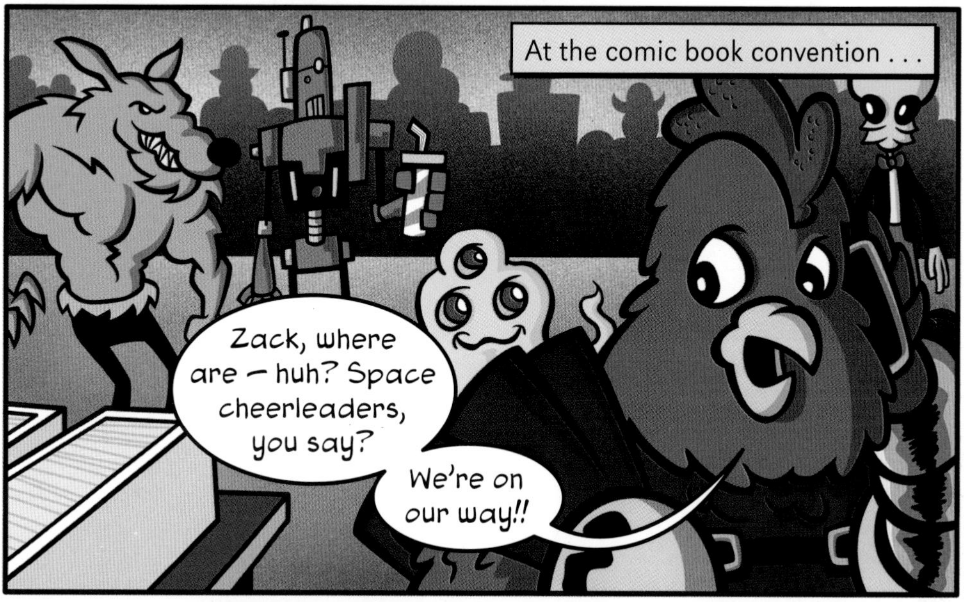
At the comic book convention . . .
Zack, where are — huh? Space cheerleaders, you say?
We're on our way!!

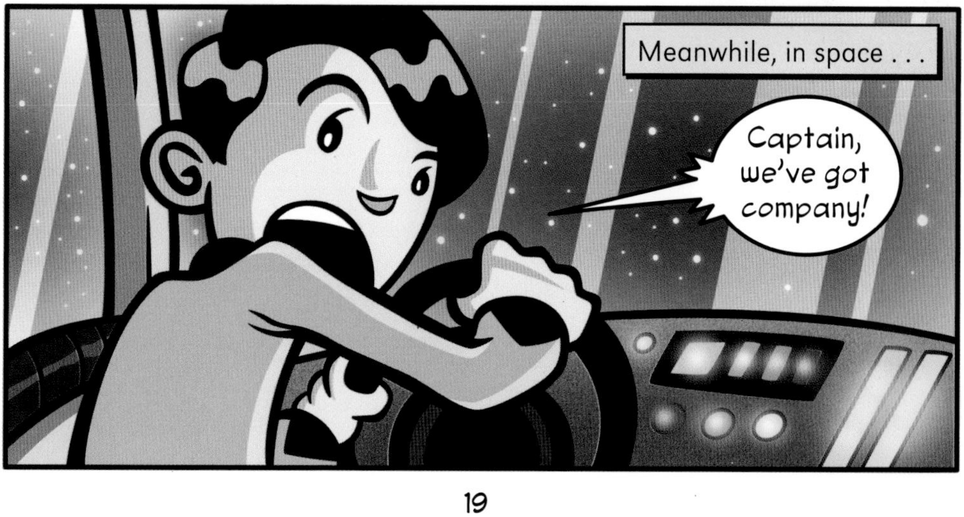
Meanwhile, in space . . .
Captain, we've got company!

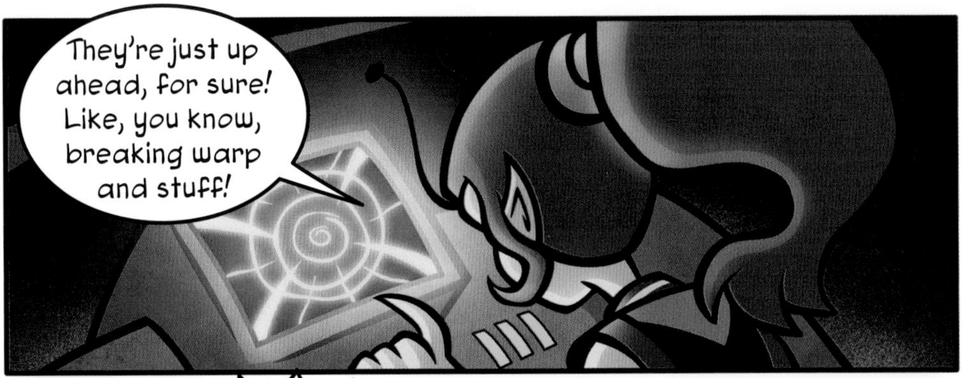
They're just up ahead, for sure! Like, you know, breaking warp and stuff!

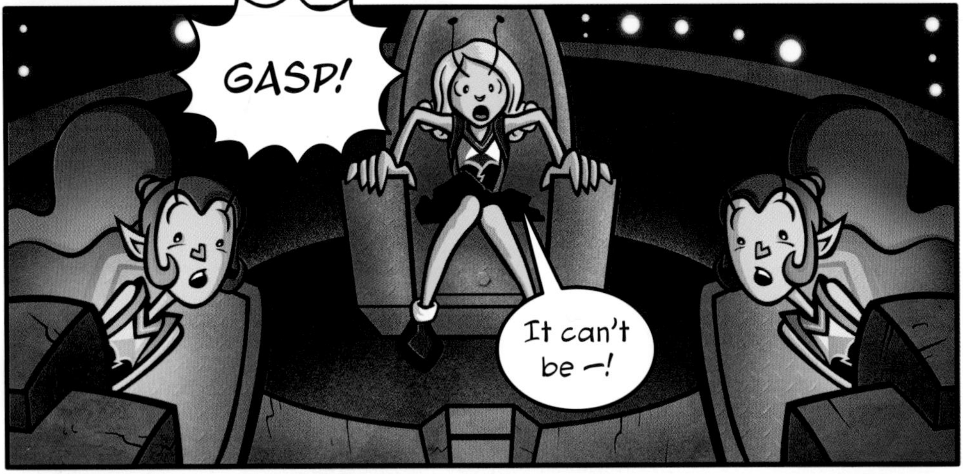
GASP!
It can't be —!

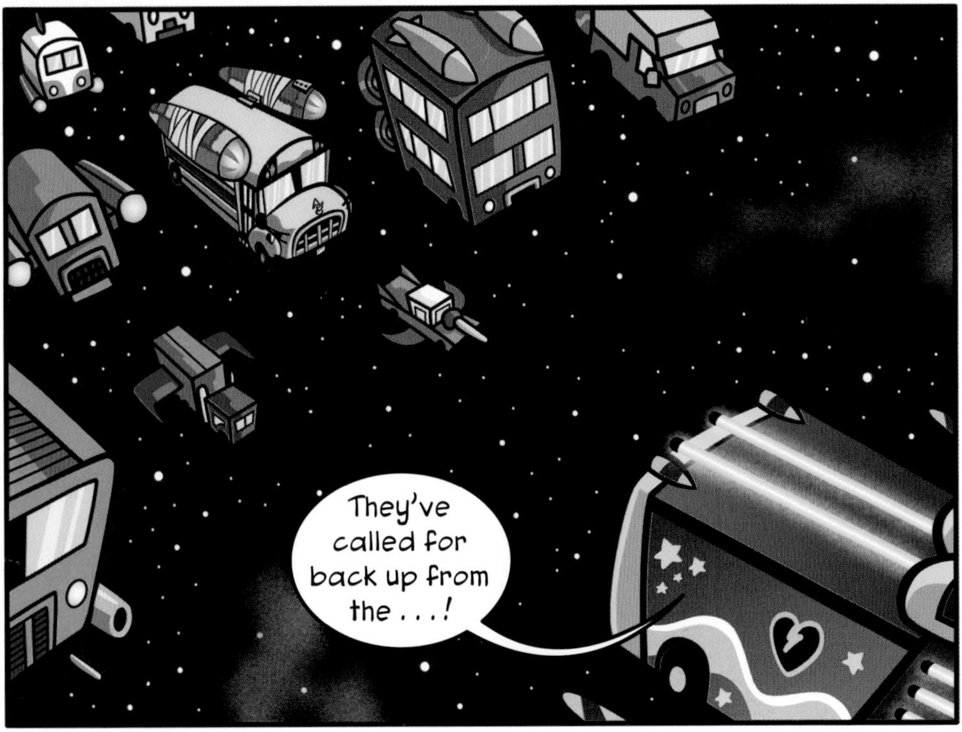
They've called for back up from the . . . !

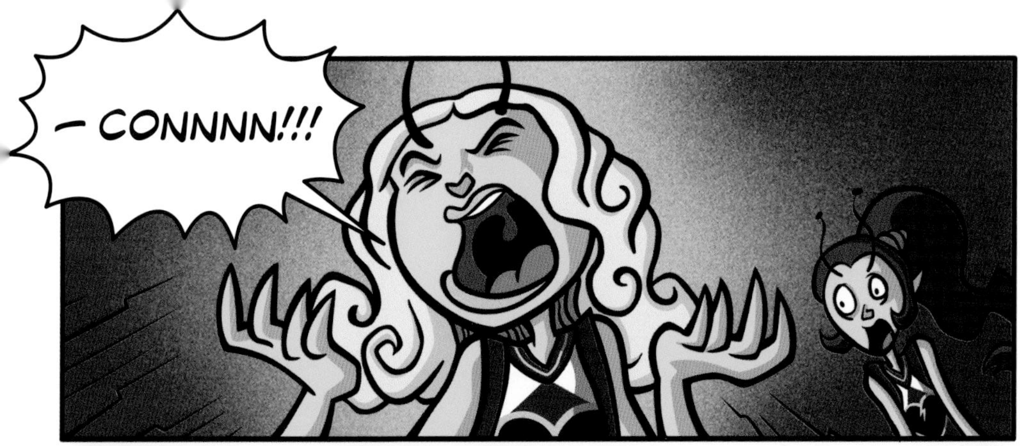
– CONNNN!!!

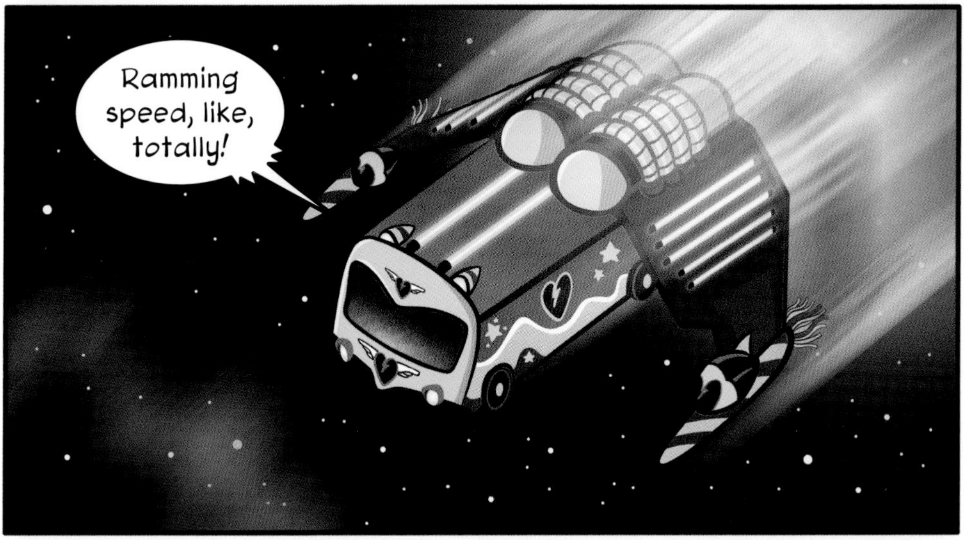
Ramming speed, like, totally!

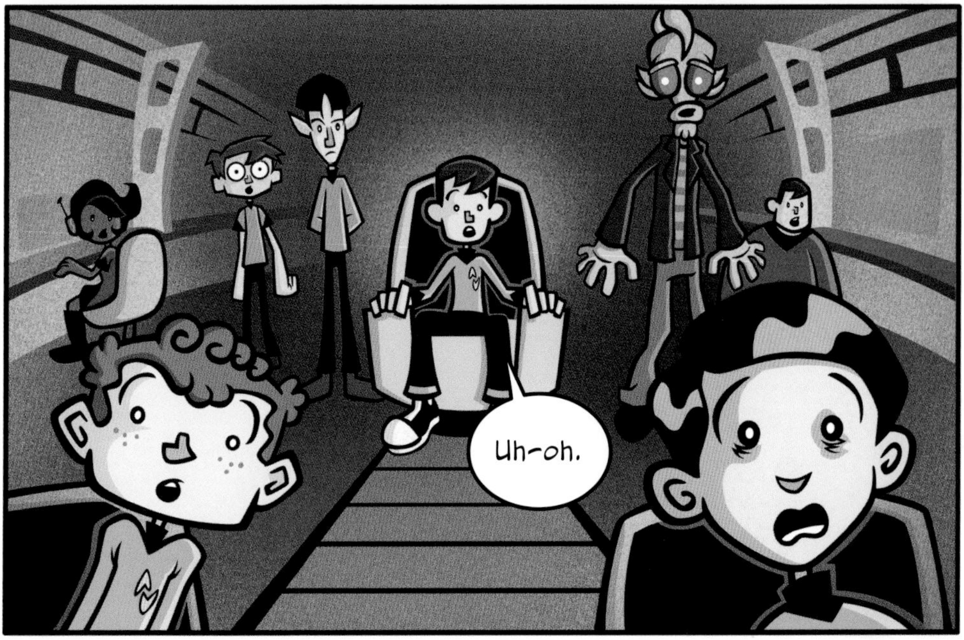
Uh-oh.

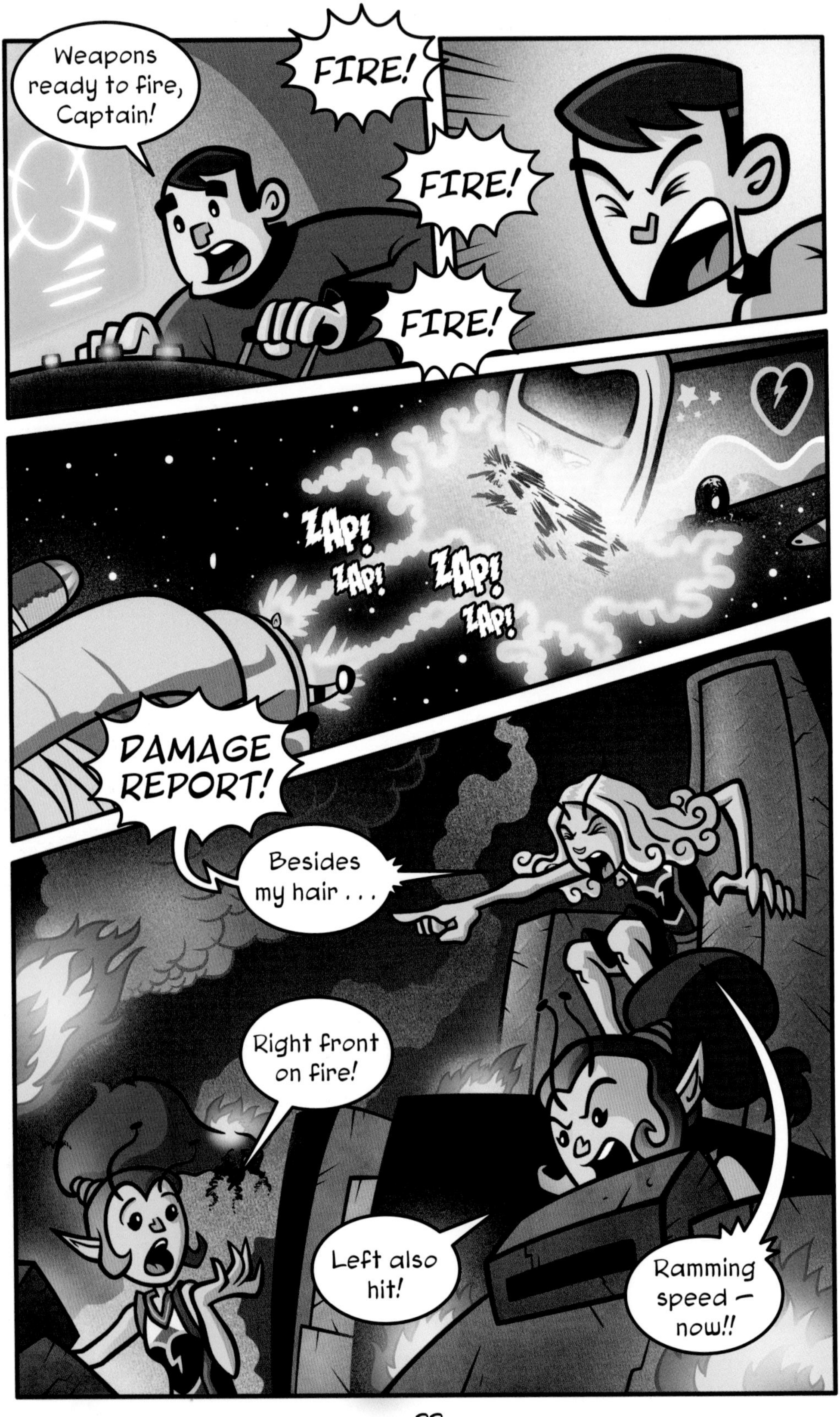
Weapons ready to fire, Captain!
FIRE!
FIRE!
FIRE!
ZAP!
ZAP!
ZAP!
ZAP!
DAMAGE REPORT!
Besides my hair . . .
Right front on fire!
Left also hit!
Ramming speed — now!!

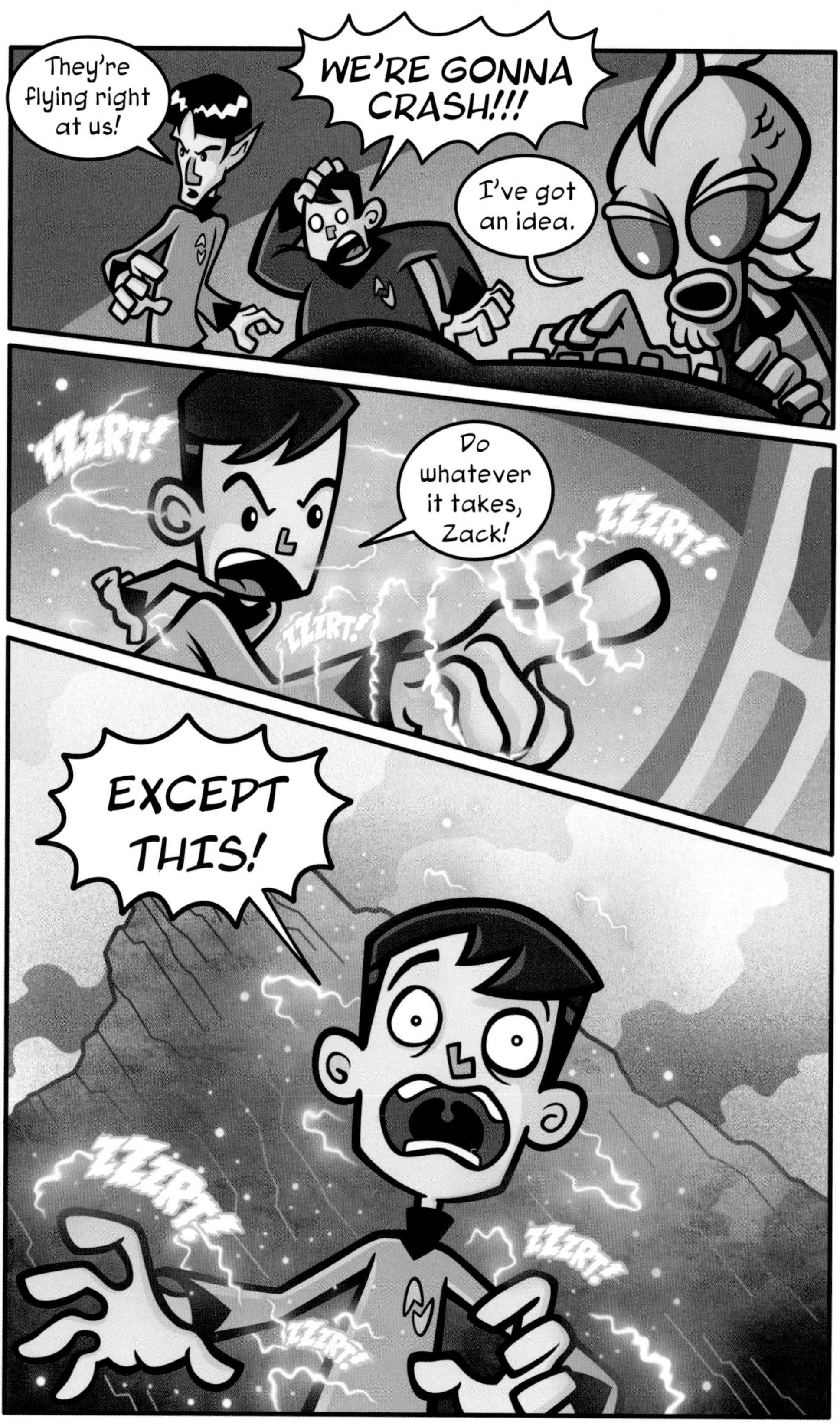
They're flying right at us!
WE'RE GONNA CRASH!!!
I've got an idea.
ZZZRT!
Do whatever it takes, Zack!
ZZZRT!
ZZZRT!
EXCEPT THIS!
ZZZRT!
ZZZRT!
ZZZRT!

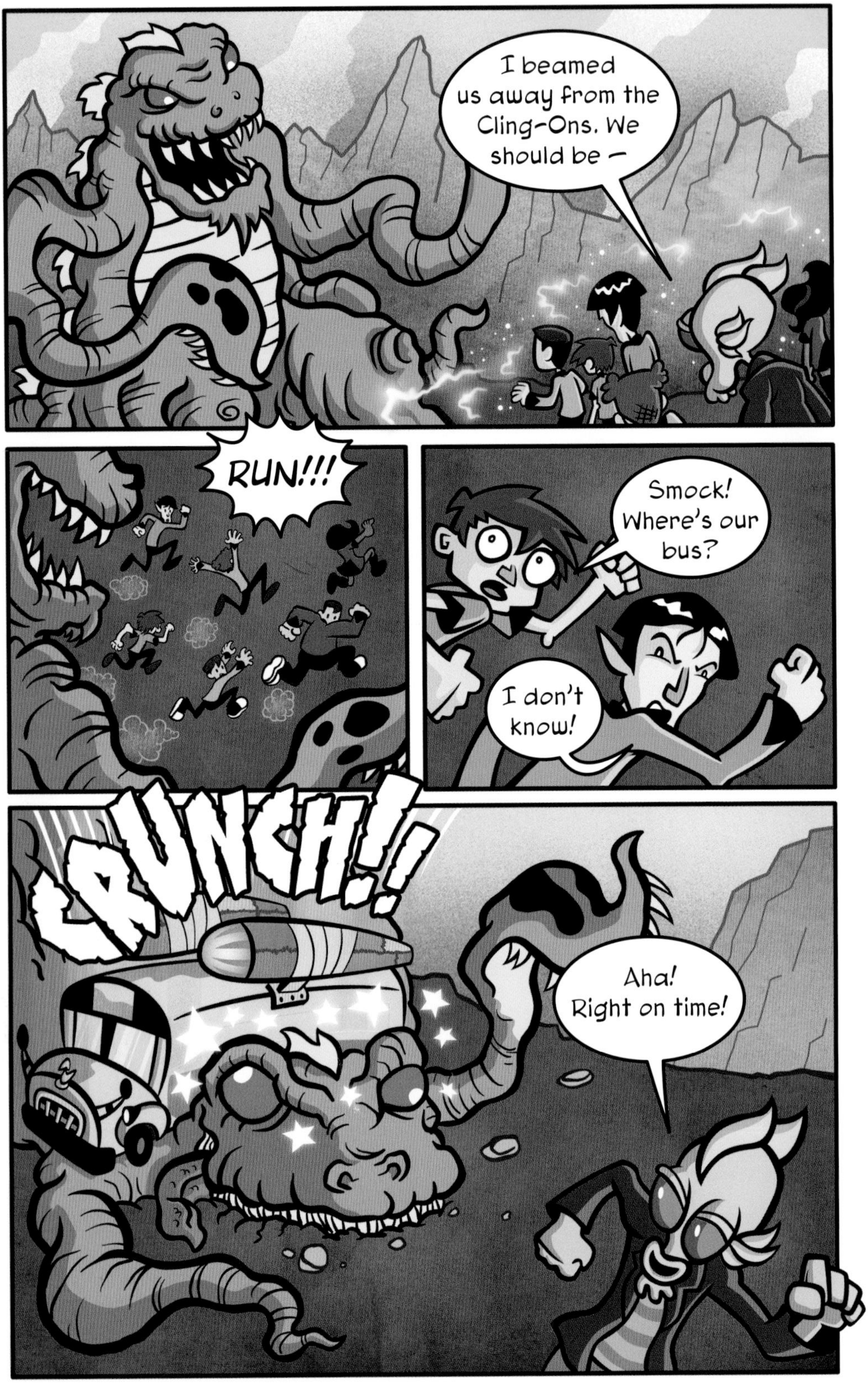
I beamed us away from the Cling-Ons. We should be —
RUN!!!
Smock! Where's our bus?
I don't know!
CRUNCH!!!
Aha! Right on time!

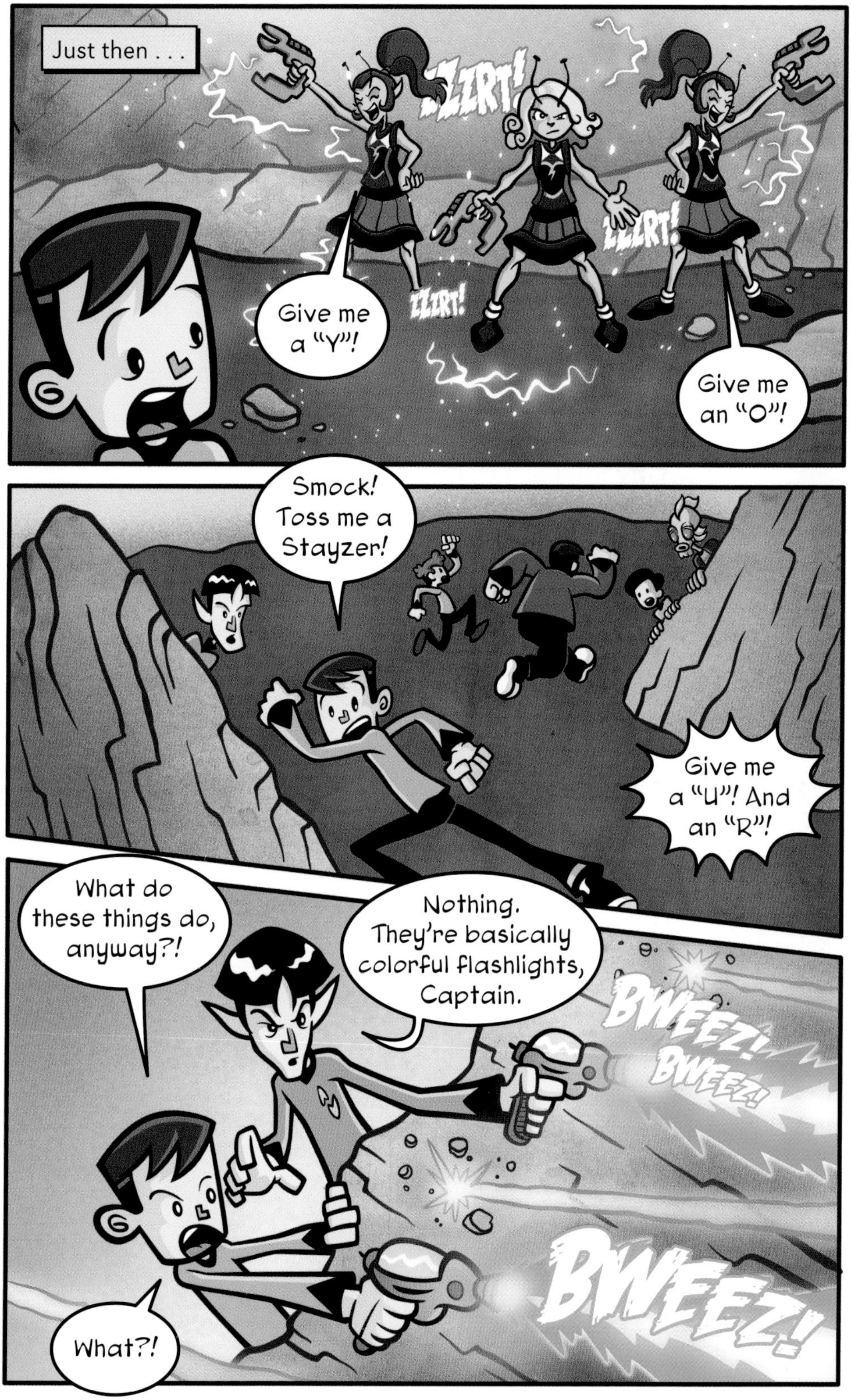
Just then . . .
ZZZRT!
Give me a "Y"!
ZZZRT!
ZZZRT!
Give me an "O"!
Smock! Toss me a Stayzer!
Give me a "U"! And an "R"!
What do these things do, anyway?!
Nothing. They're basically colorful flashlights, Captain.
BWEEZ!
BWEEZ!
BWEEZ!
What?!

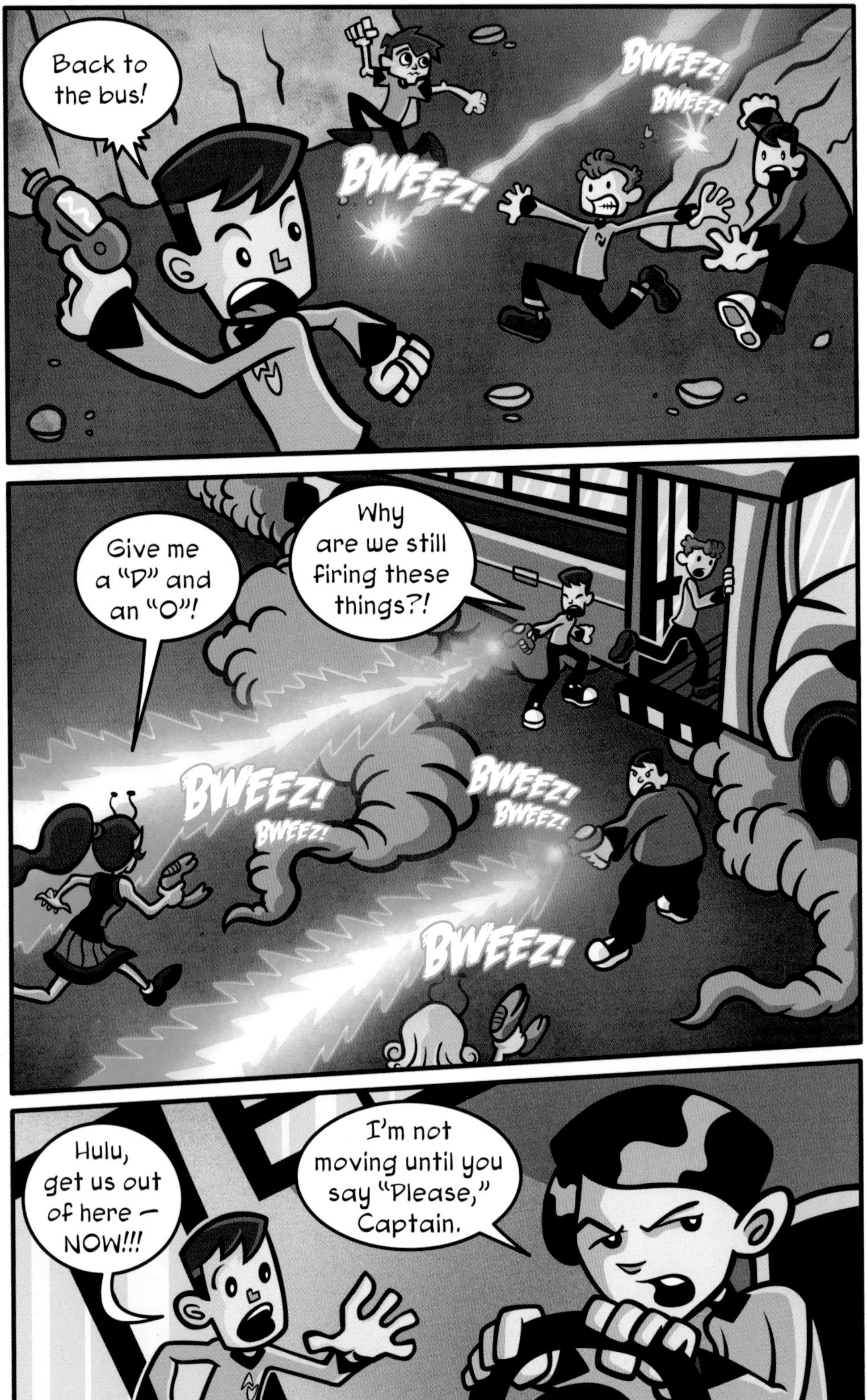

Back to the bus!
BWEEZ!
BWEEZ!
BWEEZ!
Give me a "D" and an "O"!
Why are we still firing these things?!
BWEEZ!
BWEEZ!
BWEEZ!
BWEEZ!
BWEEZ!
Hulu, get us out of here — NOW!!!
I'm not moving until you say "Please," Captain.

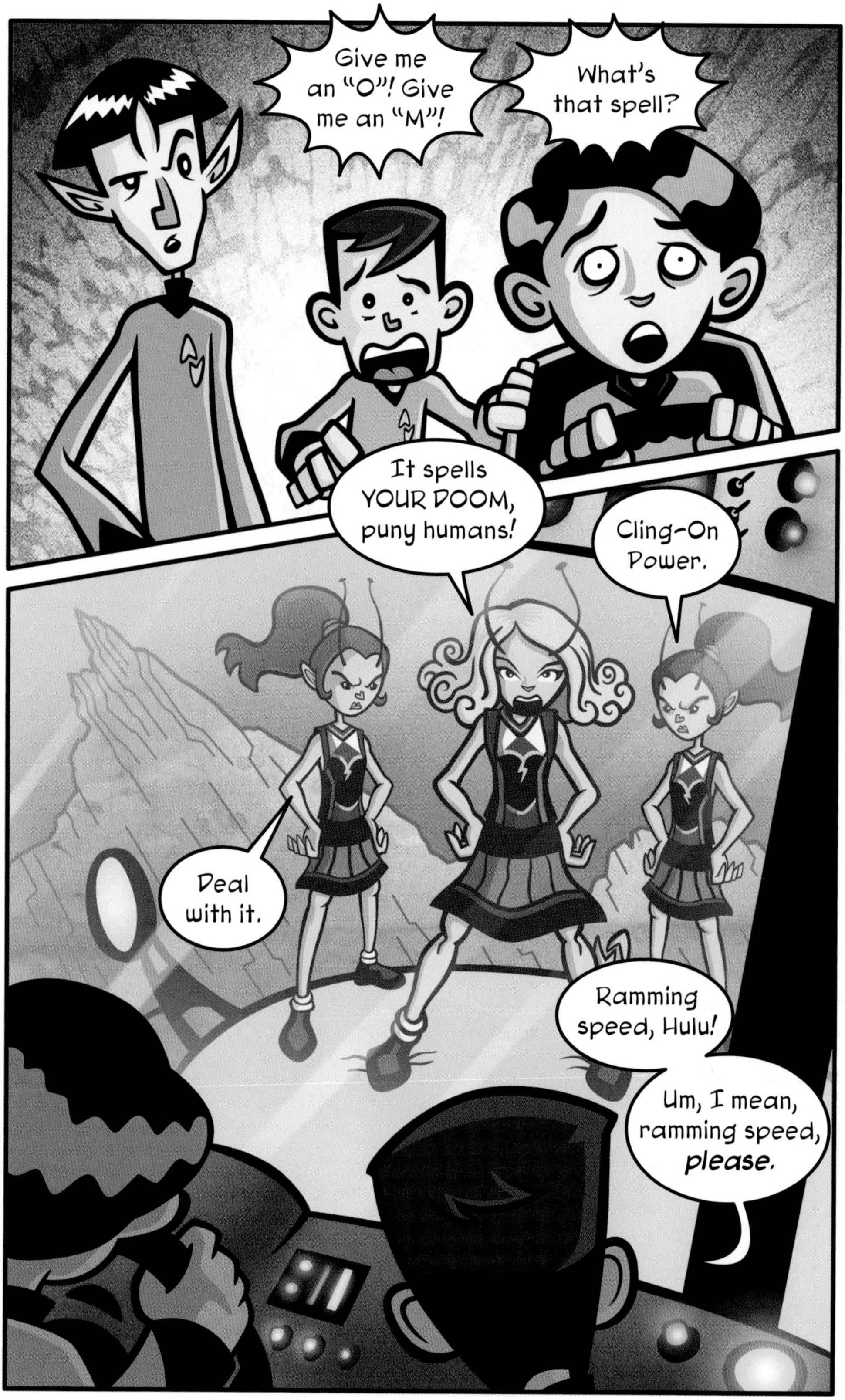
Give me an "O"! Give me an "M"!
What's that spell?
It spells YOUR DOOM, puny humans!
Cling-On Power.
Deal with it.
Ramming speed, Hulu!
Um, I mean, ramming speed, *please.*

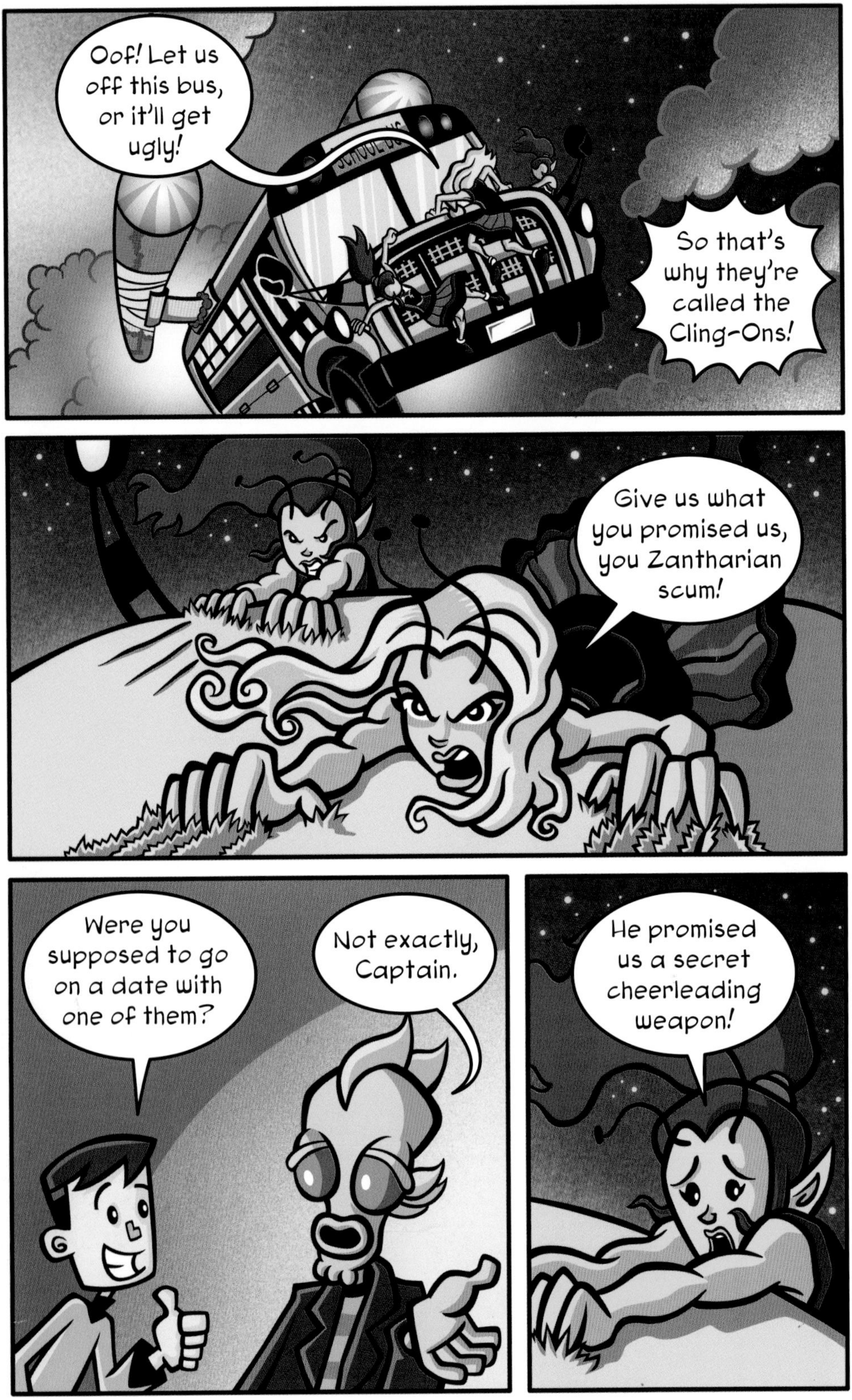
Oof! Let us off this bus, or it'll get ugly!
So that's why they're called the Cling-Ons!
Give us what you promised us, you Zantharian scum!
Were you supposed to go on a date with one of them?
Not exactly, Captain.
He promised us a secret cheerleading weapon!

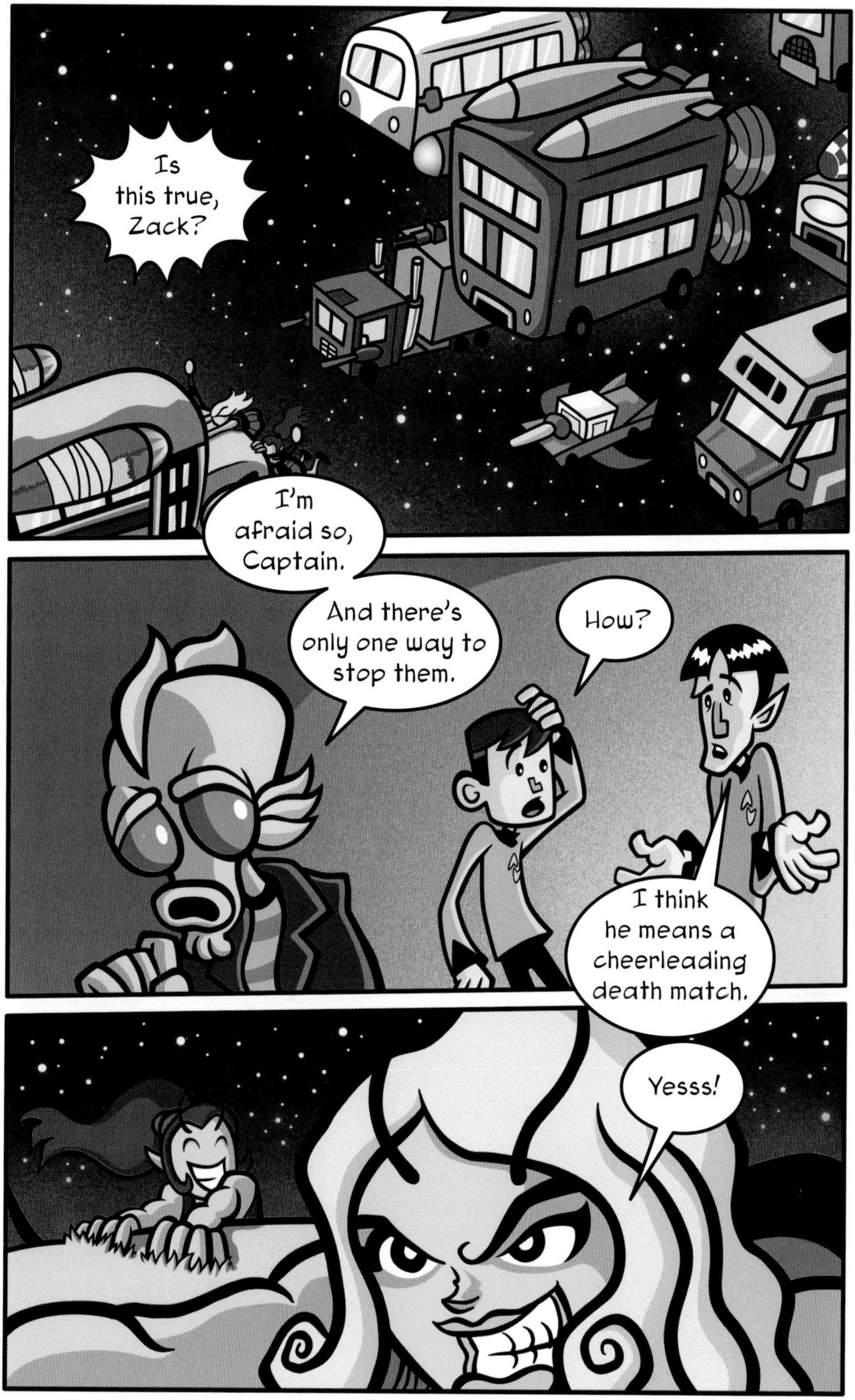
Is this true, Zack?
I'm afraid so, Captain.
And there's only one way to stop them.
How?
I think he means a cheerleading death match.
Yesss!

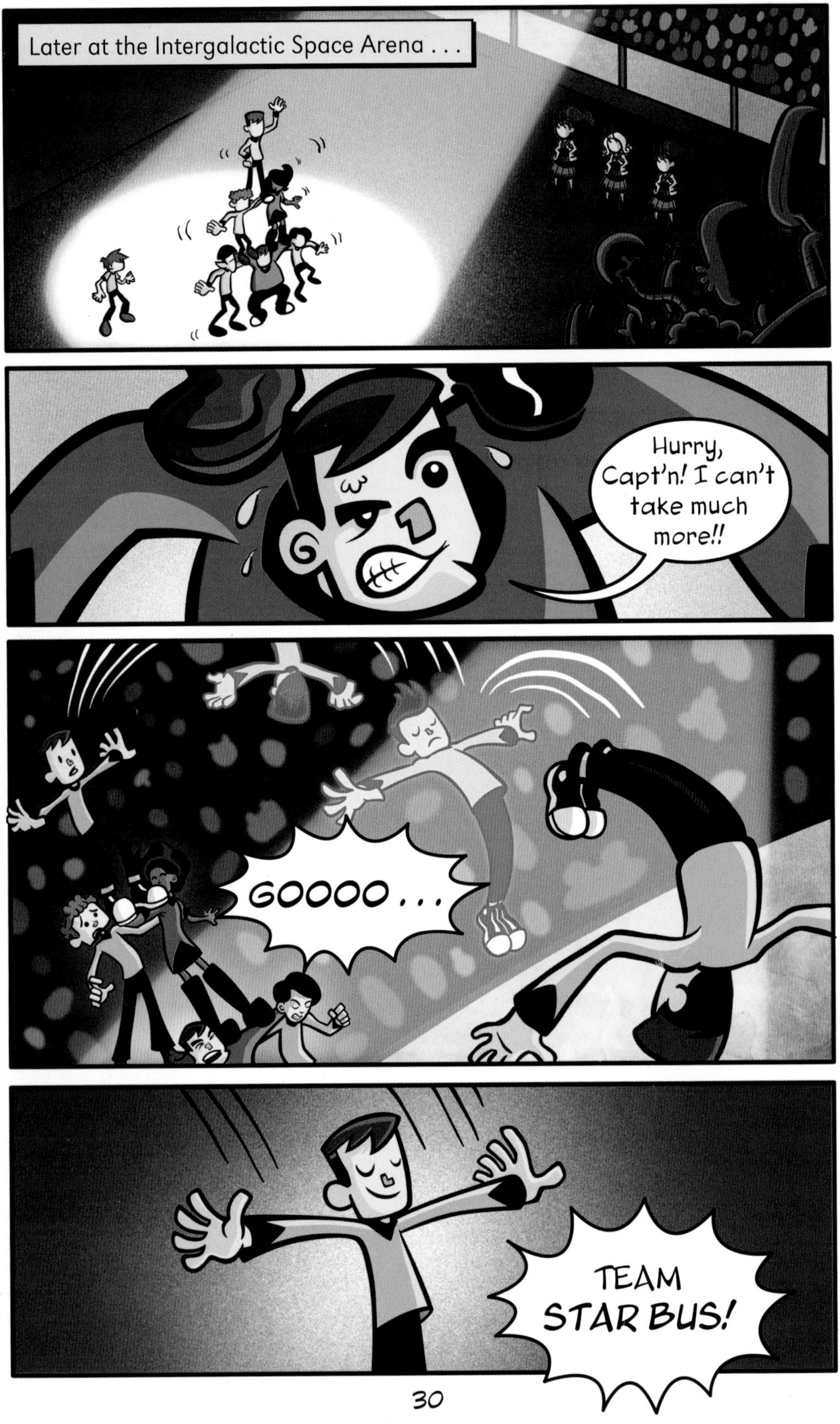
Later at the Intergalactic Space Arena . . .
Hurry, Capt'n! I can't take much more!!
GOOOO . . .
TEAM STAR BUS!

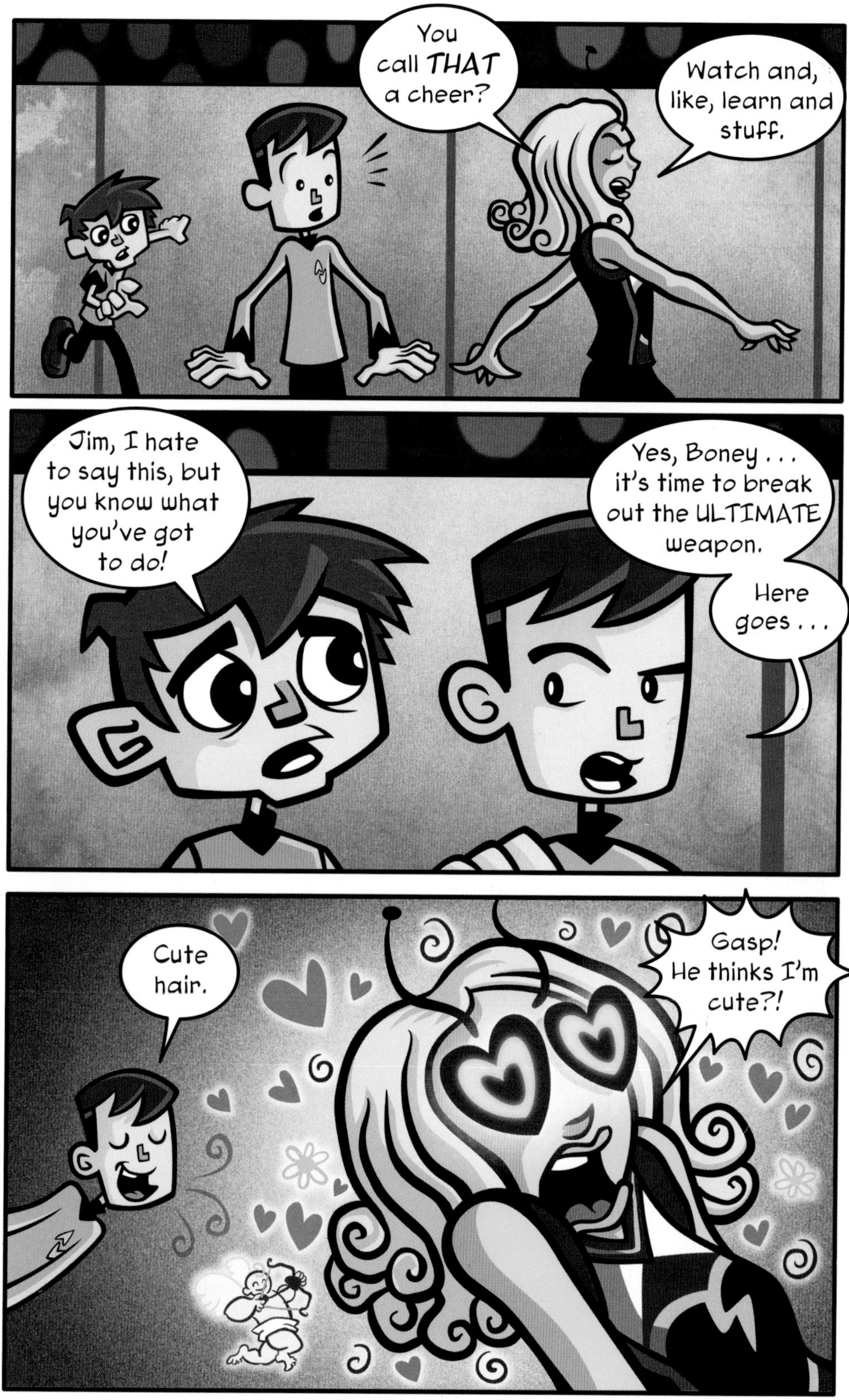
You call THAT a cheer?
Watch and, like, learn and stuff.
Jim, I hate to say this, but you know what you've got to do!
Yes, Boney . . . it's time to break out the ULTIMATE weapon.
Here goes . . .
Cute hair.
Gasp! He thinks I'm cute?!

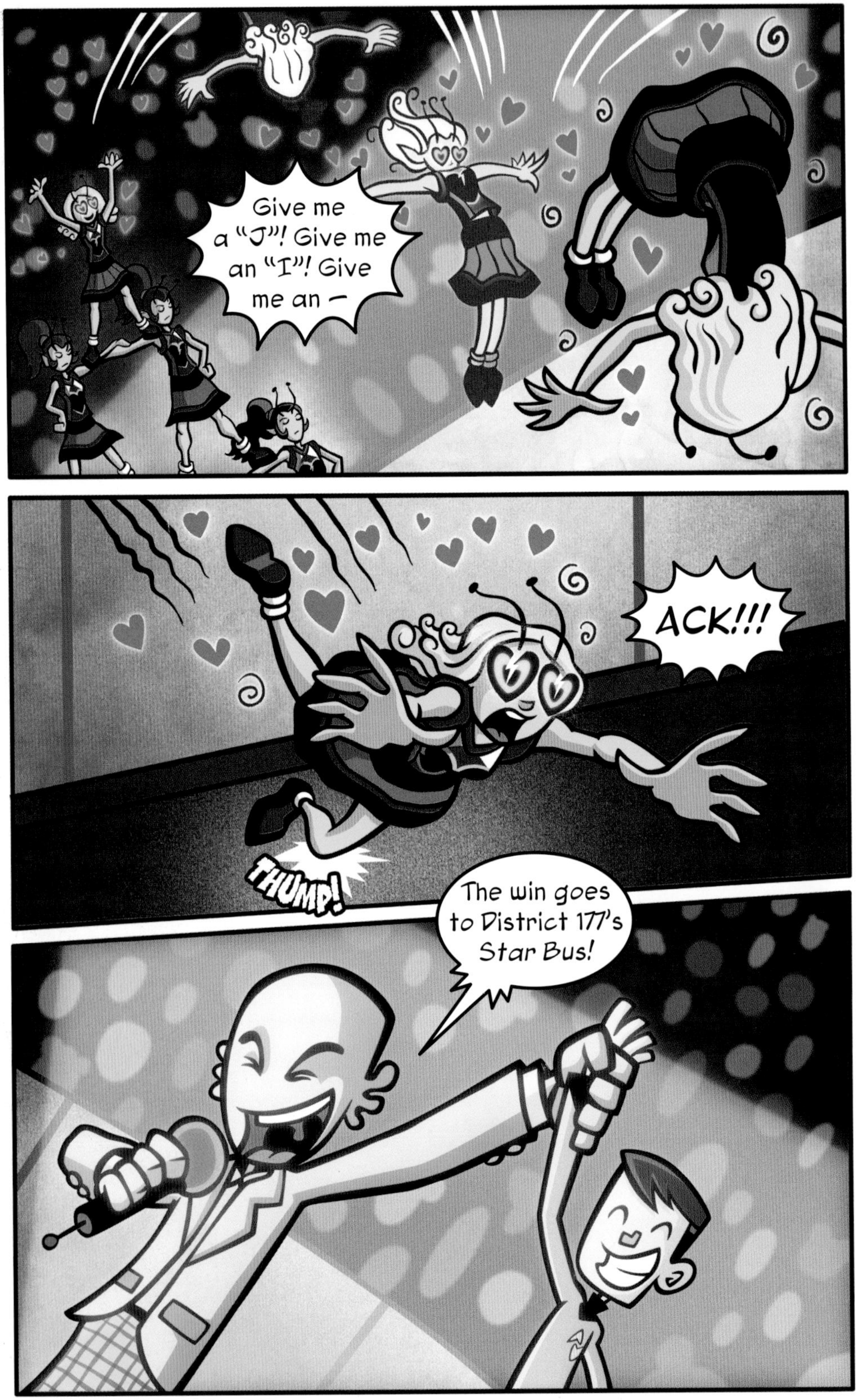
Give me a "J"! Give me an "I"! Give me an —
ACK!!!
THUMP!
The win goes to District 177's Star Bus!

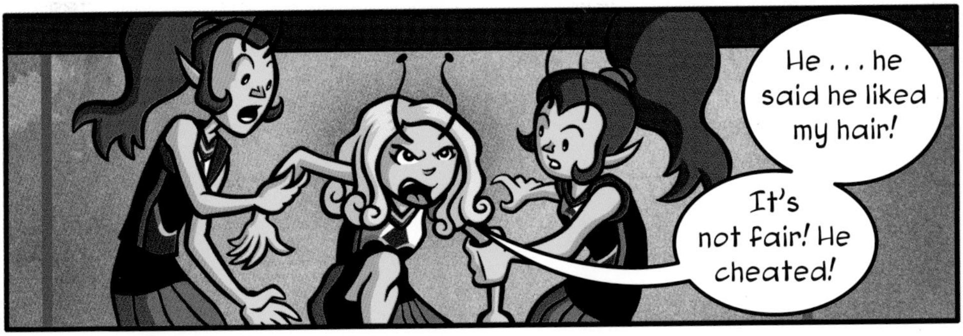
He . . . he said he liked my hair!
It's not fair! He cheated!

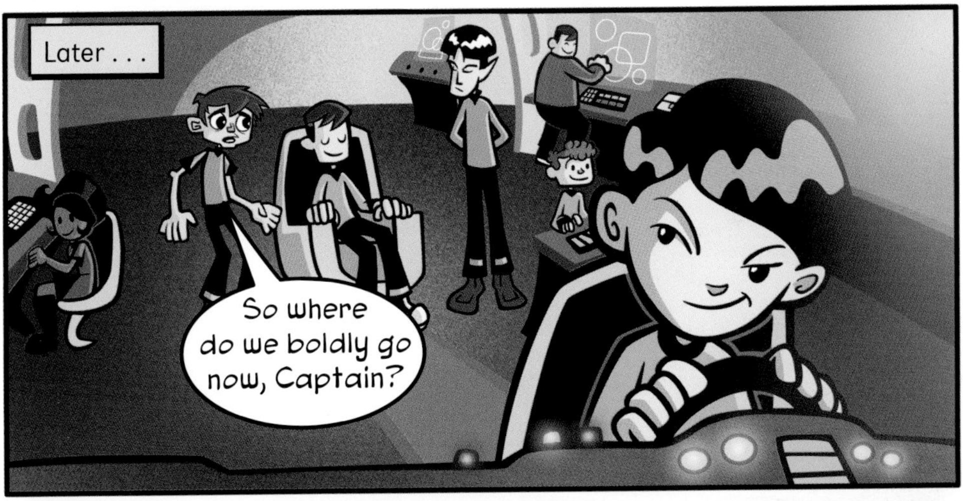
Later . . .
So where do we boldly go now, Captain?

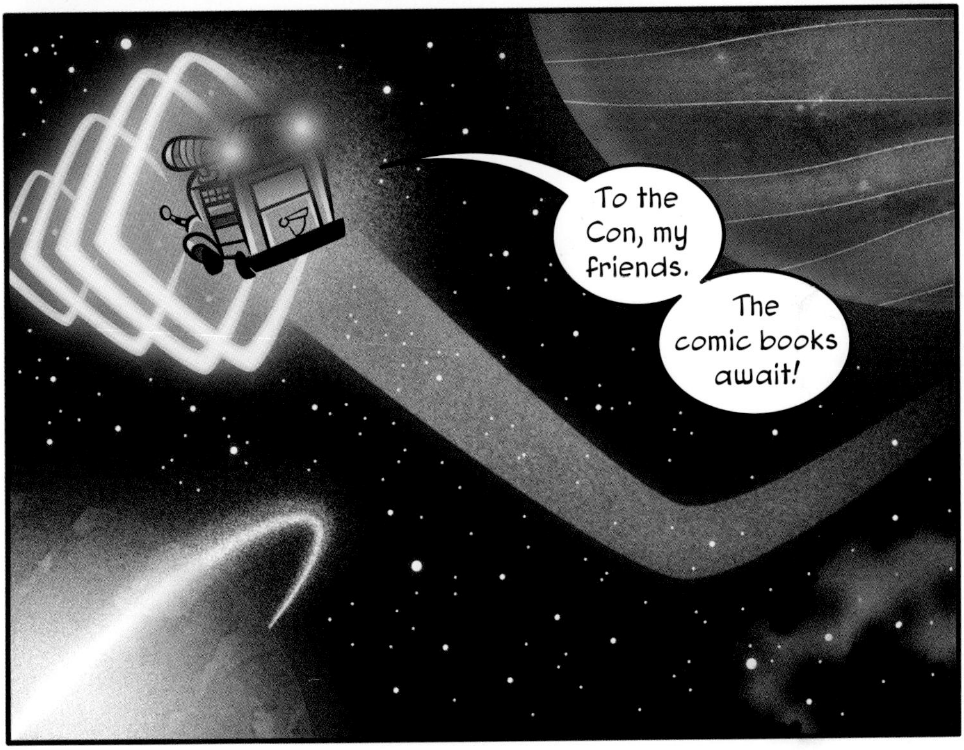
To the Con, my friends.
The comic books await!

STAR BUS

CAPTAIN CORK

Rank: Captain
Favorite planet: Earth
Special Talent: Looking like he knows what he's doing (even when he doesn't). He's also quite charming. And he's not afraid to use his secret weapon . . . his smile.

STAR BUS

SMOCK

Rank: Lieutenant Commander
Favorite planet: Vulcan
Special Talent: He can tell
what people are thinking.
He can even tell whether
someone's taken a bath!

CHECKONIT

Birthplace: Moscow, Idaho
Favorite movies: *Shout,
Scream,* and *Old Yeller*
Special Talent: He can scream
louder than an alien opera
singer with a bullhorn!

THE CLING-ONS

Favorite song: "Friends Stick
Together"
Favorite planet: Gloop in the
Great Goo Galaxy
Special Talent: These gleeful
alien cheerleaders never
give up. They're also totally
awesome. In fact, they wrote
a cheer about it:
"A-W-E, S-O-M-E! Awesome!
To-tal-ly AWESOME!!"

STAR BUS
PROFILES

AUTHOR

Scott Ciencin is a *New York Times* bestselling author of children's and adult fiction. He has written comic books, trading cards, video games, television shows, as well as many non-fiction projects. He lives in Sarasota, Florida, with his beloved wife, Denise, and his best buddy, Bear, a golden retriever. He loves writing for Stone Arch Books and is working hard on many more that are still to come.

ILLUSTRATOR

Jeff Crowther has been drawing comics for as long as he can remember. Since graduating from college, Jeff has worked on a variety of illustrations for clients including Disney, *Adventures Magazine*, and *Boy's Life Magazine*. He also wrote and illustrated the webcomic Sketchbook and has self-published several mini-comics. Jeff lives in Boardman, Ohio, with his wife, Elizabeth, and their children, Jonas and Noelle.

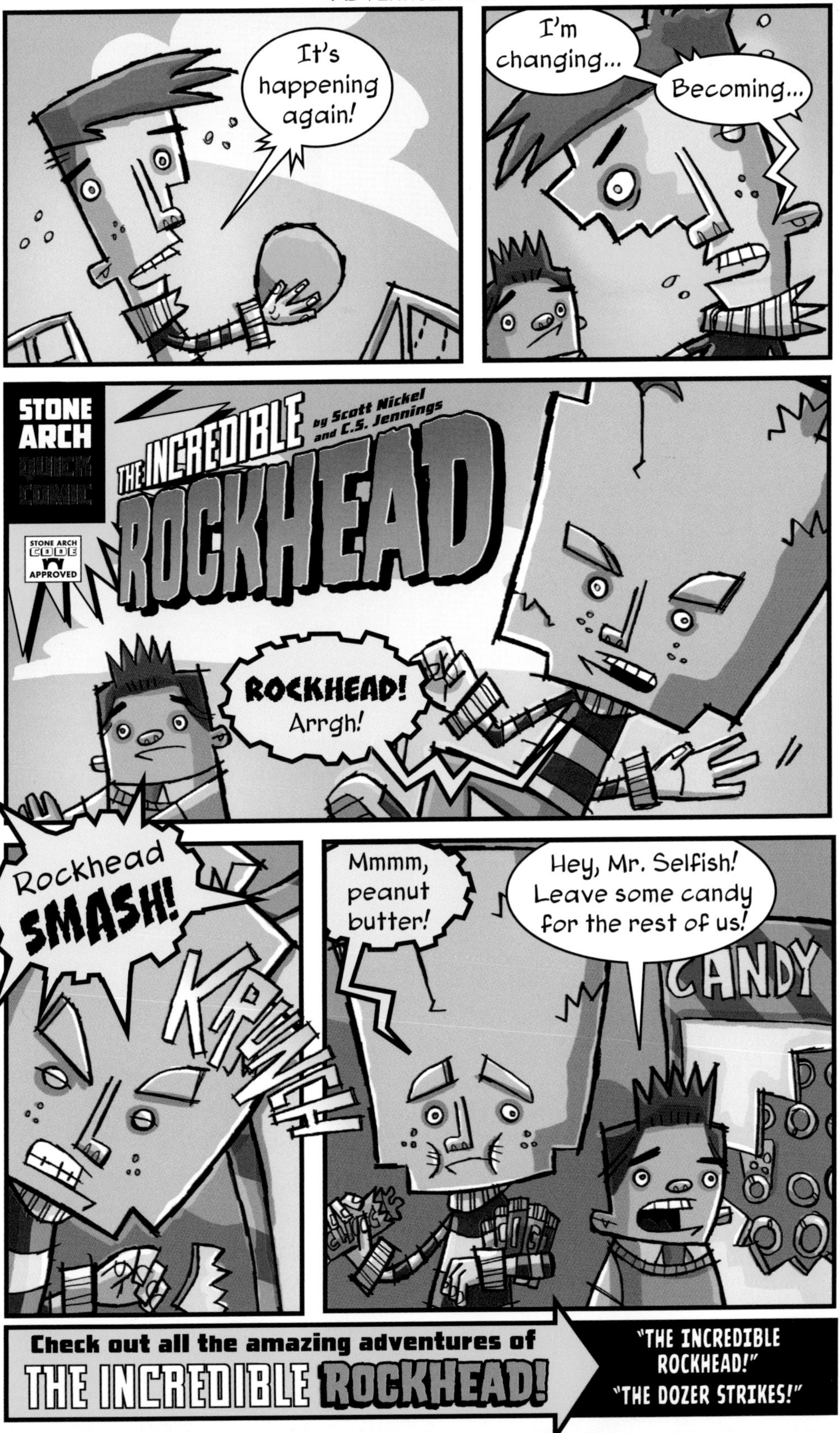
It's happening again!
I'm changing...
Becoming...
STONE ARCH
STONE ARCH CODE APPROVED
THE INCREDIBLE ROCKHEAD
by Scott Nickel and C.S. Jennings
ROCKHEAD! Arrgh!
Rockhead SMASH!
KRUNCH
Mmmm, peanut butter!
Hey, Mr. Selfish! Leave some candy for the rest of us!
CANDY
Check out all the amazing adventures of
THE INCREDIBLE ROCKHEAD!
"THE INCREDIBLE ROCKHEAD!"
"THE DOZER STRIKES!"

QUESTIONS AND PROMPTS

DISCUSSION QUESTIONS

WRITING PROMPTS

Discussion Questions

1. The crew members of the *Star Bus* worked together as a team. Have you ever been on a team or in a group? How did you work with other members to succeed?

2. If you owned a *Star Bus* and could travel anywhere in the universe, where would you go? Would you fly to the nearest star? Would you land on Mars? Discuss your outer-space trip.

Writing Prompts

1. What do you think will happen next? Write another story about the crew members of the *Star Bus*. What adventures do they have? Who do they meet? Write about it!

2. Write a story about an everyday object that turns into a high-tech vehicle. What if the fridge became a shuttle, or the tub became a submarine? Describe your homemade craft.

GLOSSARY

boldly (BOHLD-lee)—with confidence and without fear of danger

convention (kuhn-VEN-shuhn)—a large gathering of people who have the same interests

destruction (di-STRUHK-shun)—the act of destroying or ruining something completely

doom (DOOM)—a terrible fate usually ending in death

duel (DOO-uhl)—a fight between two people

empire (EM-pire)—a nation that is ruled by an emperor or empress

familiar (fuh-MIL-yur)—well-known or easily recognized

transform (transs-FORM)—to make a great change

ultimate (UHL-tuh-mit)—greatest or best

warp speed (WORP SPEED)—the highest possible speed

STONE ARCH BOOKS™

Published in 2011
A Capstone Imprint
151 Good Counsel Drive, P.O. Box 669
Mankato, Minnesota 56002
www.capstonepub.com

Cataloging-in-Publication Data is available at the Library of Congress website.

ISBN: 918-1-4342-2637-2 (library binding)
ISBN: 978-1-4342-3067-6 (paperback)

Summary: The *Star Bus* is about to go where all good geeks have gone before . . . a comic book convention!

Designer: Brann Garvey
Art Director: Bob Lentz
Editor: Donald Lemke
Assoc. Editor: Sean Tulien
Production Specialist: Michelle Biedscheid
Creative Director: Heather Kindseth
Editorial Director: Michael Dahl
Publisher: Lori Benton

Printed in the United States of America
in Stevens Point, Wisconsin.
092010
005934WZS11